Natália Gomes has an M

writing fiction with a ... as ...mental health amo...g young adults. Her debut novel *Dear Charlie* is endorsed by Amnesty International and was longlisted for the 2018 International Dublin Literary Award.

Natália currently lives in Scotland with her chocolate labrador Charlie, and is completing a PhD in English Studies.

If you want to get in touch, follow Natália on Twitter @nd_gomes and on Instagram @ndgomes

We Are Not Okay

Natália Gomes

ONE PLACE. MANY STORIES

This novel is entirely a work of fiction. The names, characters
and incidents portrayed in it are the work of the author's
imagination. Any resemblance to actual persons, living or
dead, events or localities is entirely coincidental.

HQ
An imprint of HarperCollins*Publishers* Ltd
1 London Bridge Street
London SE1 9GF

This paperback edition 2019

1
First published in Great Britain by
HQ, an imprint of HarperCollins*Publishers* Ltd 2019

ISBN PB: 978-0-00-829184-6

MIX
Paper from
responsible sources
FSC™ C007454

This book is produced from independently certified FSC™ paper
to ensure responsible forest management.

For more information visit: www.harpercollins.co.uk/green

Printed and bound in Great Britain by
CPI Group (UK) Ltd, Croydon, CR0 4YY

This book is dedicated to the numerous campaigns and charities that challenge us on how we think and speak about sexual violence and bullying.

#WeAreNotOkay Songlist

DAUGHTER–Youth

CIVIL WARS & TAYLOR SWIFT–Safe & Sound

JOY WILLIAMS–Don't Let Me Down

GABRIELLE APLIN–Please Don't Say You Love Me

PHOEBE BRIDGERS–Georgia

FOXES–Devil Side

CHVRCHES–The Mother We Share

STAVES–Make it Holy

BROODS–Worth the Fight

LANA DEL REY–Love

PHOEBE BRIDGERS–Smoke Signals

JAPANESE HOUSE–Face Like Thunder

LORDE–Yellow Flicker Beat

DAUGHTER–Home

BIRDY–Wild Horses

PHOEBE BRIDGERS–Motion Sickness

BROODS–Heartlines

*THE WIND AND THE WAVE–It's a Longer Road to California
Than I Thought*

SMITH & THELL–Statues

BIRDY–Wings

SOPHIA

His fingers graze my lips. Inside I explode.

His hand reaches behind my neck and scoops a handful of my hair. Tipping my head back slightly, he kisses my neck.

I grip the edge of the bed, clutching a handful of the floral quilt cover. My other hand slides up his torso, over his navy T-shirt, and up to his head. I pull him in closer and feel a churning in my belly. When his lips find mine again, the butterflies disappear.

Everything about him is familiar but new at the same time.

He brushes a stray strand off my face and loops it between his fingers.

I don't know where his other hand is until I feel it on the belt loop of my jeans, then it's on my stomach.

My body lurches. I don't like his hand there. He must feel that loose saggy skin around my middle, the curve of my belly after a big meal, the fat.

I scoot my body to the side, away from his hand.

'Are you OK?' he whispers.

If I draw attention to it then he'll be thinking about it, like me. I'll be unattractive to him. Disgusting. So I just nod and then pull him in again so he forgets what just happened.

He presses harder against my lips, then slides his hand back over my stomach but this time he moves it before I have a chance to. He's moving it upwards though and now it's at the edge of the cardigan around my shoulders. He shimmies it off my shoulder and I shift my weight slightly to let him bring it down around my elbows. My green vest with the lace scalloped trim is exposed. It's really a PJ top – well, one half of a shorts set from Next that I got for my birthday one year. It's not supposed to be a top. *He's* not supposed to see it. But he is. And I'm letting him.

Outside, rain beats hard on the window pane, pushing its way into our space, our moment. The wind cries and howls. It wants in. And for a moment – a brief fleeting moment – I think I want out. But then that thought passes or is forced out of my mind because I don't want out. I want to be here with Steve. With my boyfriend. I'm just scared. It's moving too fast. I'm not ready. But he is.

I stretch out my hand awkwardly, my arm still caught in the fabric of my cardigan, to tap on the music on my phone. I've created a playlist for us with all of our favourite songs but also some new ones. I hope he likes it. I spent time working on it last night, probably when I should have been finishing my physics homework but this seemed more important to me.

It is important.

What we have is important.

I love Steve.

But I can't reach my phone without moving my body out from under him and I don't want to do that. Not just yet. But then his hand is suddenly under my vest, under my bra, and I have to.

Because that's it. Right there. That's my ceiling. He just hit it.

My hand cups his and I push it off my body back down to his side. He tries again. So I move the hand away, again.

And again.

And then again.

'Steve,' I finally say, sitting upright. I slide my body out from under him and press my spine against the headboard.

He sits up too and kneels on one leg. He sighs deeply and I wish I could give him exactly what he wants, be exactly what he needs. But I can't. At least not now. Not tonight. My parents are going to be back any minute, I'm wearing jeans, I can't remember the colour of my underwear let alone whether it matches my bra. Although I'm ninety per cent sure it doesn't. Maybe even ninety-eight per cent.

I've thought about it. Of course I've thought about it. I'm seventeen years old. What seventeen-year-old with a boyfriend hasn't thought about their first time? But I haven't prepared. I need time to prepare. I need my playlist. I need candles, the curtains closed, the dirty laundry basket out of that corner, the coffee mug from breakfast off my dresser, that bronzer stain by my mirror gone, half a stone vanished from my midriff, this spot on my chin completely obliterated, and preferably knickers that aren't from Primark and that my mum didn't buy me for Christmas last year.

But I can't tell him that.

So instead I scrunch up my face and hope my cheeks aren't burning as red as I think they are. Which they probably are.

He sighs even deeper, even louder. 'Not tonight then?' he finally asks, looking up at me.

I lightly touch his left cheek feeling the stubble sharp against my fingertips. 'Not tonight.'

He takes another deep breath and again I wonder what he's thinking inside. Is he getting sick of waiting? Is he getting bored with me? Does he still fancy me?

I lean in and wrap my arms around him, pulling him in again. When our lips part, his face has relaxed a little and the lines around his eyes are now almost completely faded from his skin. He looks less tense. He brushes another strand off my cheek and tucks it behind my ear.

4

His fingers linger over the silver and pearl studs in my earlobe, before dropping heavily to the bed. 'OK.' He swings his legs off the bed and puts his face in his hands, leaning over. Away from me.

I've disappointed him.

I hate doing that, but I keep doing it. Why?

I swing a leg around him and lay my head gently on his back. 'I'm sorry,' I whisper in his ear.

'It's fine, Soph, really. We've got plenty of time. And it'll happen, right?'

Lifting my head, I wrap my arms around him and interlace my fingers at his stomach. I pull him in closer. 'Of course it'll happen.' I playfully press against his belly until he squirms.

He laughs and wriggles away. He runs a hand through his hair and then turns to face me. He places a hand on my cheek. 'Soon, yeah?'

I push my cheek further into his palm and press a smile onto my face even though I don't feel it inside. 'Yes, soon. I promise.'

He kisses me again, quickly and briefly this time. Then leans back over the bed.

'You're leaving?' I ask, watching him shove his feet into his trainers.

'Yeah, your mum and dad will be home soon anyway. And I promised Lee I'd catch up with him tonight.'

'Oh.' I turn and look at the chrome-rimmed clock

on my wall, where the hands extend out from the Eiffel Tower and slowly circle around an outline of Paris by day. 'Now? It's kinda late?'

He fixes his laces then turns to me. 'I'll text you.'

He tries to move but I grab his torso and pull him into me. I wrap my arms around his neck and kiss him again. When I pull away, his eyes are already open. 'Don't forget to text me.'

He smiles, playfully nuzzles against my nose then walks out of the bedroom, leaving the door open. A cold draught seeps in from the hallway and snakes up to my bed, to my bare shoulders and exposed arms. I fling my body back onto the quilt and listen to his footsteps. His feet get quieter as he moves through to the back of the house and out the rear door.

And then he's gone.

The cold air lingers in the room, encasing me, squeezing me. My fingers scroll through my iPhone until our last conversation.

Can't wait to see you tonight x

He'd sent that to me only an hour before he'd arrived. It was enough to send warmth to my cheeks and whole body. I'd waited for him.

Steve and I have been together for a year now, although I can't believe it's been a whole year. I guess time really does fly by when you're this happy. I still remember when I first noticed him. It feels like it was last night. I didn't even like him at first. He was overconfident, brash, even a little rude at times. We didn't fall into the same social circle, not that I run in a particular 'social circle'. I've always struggled in social situations. I get nervous when people talk to me, wondering what they're expecting me to say back and what happens if my response doesn't meet their expectations. What if I'm not funny enough? Or not interesting enough? What if they're not even talking to me and instead they're actually talking to the person behind me?

All these scenarios play out in my head to the point where going out is no longer an option. All I want to do is go to school, finish my homework, and spend all my free time with Steve. I have friends of course. Well, maybe just one. I hang out with Ulana a lot. Her boyfriend plays football with Steve on Thursday nights and Saturday mornings. She can't ever watch him play though. She's not supposed to have a boyfriend. Her parents are crazy strict.

But I don't freeze up so much when I'm around her, and never with Steve. I can be myself completely with him. I never have to worry if I'm funny enough or interesting enough. I never have to look over my shoulder when he talks because he's always talking to me. Steve doesn't care about my social skills or my ability – or inability – to work a room full of people. He does all that for me. He speaks for me when we go out so I never have to think too much about what to say. Honestly, it's not the social expectations of dating that terrify me. It's not even the anxiety-producing process of getting prepared to sleep with your boyfriend for the first time. It's the simple truth – that was revealed to me only recently – that for him, this isn't his first time. He's done this before. Probably many times before based on what Ulana told me last week. Steve is experienced in this sort of stuff.

And me?

Well, I am clearly not.

I don't know what I'm doing. I'm so lost when it comes to relationships. I'm not like the other girls at school, and definitely nothing like the girls he's dated. I'm not social and fun like Trina Davis. She's the life of the party. Yes, she's usually throwing up in someone's garden by the end of the night, but she still tops me. And Lucy McNeil?

No one is like Lucy McNeil.

I'll never be as confident, or as pretty, and certainly never as popular, as <u>Lucy McNeil</u>.

LUCY

'I had an amazing summer,' I start. Immediately all three girls lean in to give me their complete attention. I would be a little mad if they didn't. It's a good story. Mine usually are. 'I went to Italy with my mum and dad in July for three weeks then Mallorca in August.'

(The Mallorca part is true).

'You look so tanned. I'm so jealous!' cried Mollie, raising her sandwich to her pink-stained lips.

'I know. I'm so scared it's already fading though,' I say, puckering my mouth into a sulk. I hold out my arm, still golden brown as if I only came back yesterday. No one needs to know I spent most of last week on the sunbed. It has to look like I spent most of July in Italy. It has to look like I'm telling the truth. Otherwise, they'll know.

'You should use Boots' Extender Tan. I slathered that on after I went to Florida last summer and it really worked,' Cara said, stretching out her arm to meet mine.

'Have you seen Rhys since you got back?' Lily suddenly asks.

Cara nudges her in the side of her stomach.

'I didn't mean to bring him up. I was just wondering if you were getting back together?'

I take a deep breath and look back over my shoulder to make sure he's not nearby. 'Well, we did see each other a bit over the summer—'

'Really? Because I heard he saw Trina Davis quite a bit over the summer too?'

I give Mollie a stare so hard that her eyes water slightly. She swallows hard and I can tell by her expression that a piece of bread went down a little too rough. But she can't reach for her SmartWater yet. Not until I'm finished with my staredown.

OK, now I'm done.

'I don't even want to hear her name,' I say. 'Whatever happened over the summer was clearly because Rhys was heartbroken over me. That girl is walking around like they were dating or something.'

'But they are, aren't they? That's what Rhys told Steve.'

My insides start to burn. 'Steve's a liar. Besides, if they were they're not now. And he was probably not the only boy she was seeing—'

'Wait, so they were dating? Like, *dating* dating?' Mollie

edges in closer. Her lip gloss is a shade too light for her skin tone. And she has an ugly pimple on her forehead. But I don't tell her that.

'No, Mollie. But she clearly thinks they were. What she doesn't know is that Rhys has been texting me.'

'I knew it! Tell us more,' urges Lily.

'Well, it's not official yet but we're talking again and that's a good sign.' I push the cucumber around in my salad bowl, wondering whether I should tell them about the other guy in July. But when I look up I see their little eager faces desperate for more information, more gossip, so I bite my lip. They wouldn't understand. They might judge me. They might not even believe me. 'I was the one who broke up with him, remember?' That's another lie. 'But he's enjoying playing a little hard to get, which is fine for now.'

'Boys,' Cara shrugs. Apparently her only contribution to the conversation.

'Boys,' Lily seconds.

Mollie is too busy fishing for the piece of arugula in her molar.

I glance around the lunchroom at Birchwood High School. It seems different this year. We all seem different this year. Maybe it's not them. Maybe it's only me that's changed.

This is going to be a good year.
This is going to be a good year.

If I keep saying it, it will make it true. Isn't that how it works? Positive thinking, blah, blah.

Then I see her.

Throwing her head back, laughing, mouth wide. She's walking with another girl in our year, whose name I either always forget or never knew to begin with.

'Did you see who just walked in?' Mollie asks.

'She's walking our way, Luce,' Cara adds.

She edges closer to our table.

'Do something,' Lily urges me.

'Slut,' I cough out, throwing my hand up to my mouth. The word feels funny on my tongue, tastes bitter. But the girls giggle and I smile with them.

Trina stops and turns around, her limp mousy blonde hair sliding greasily over a shoulder. 'What did you say?'

'Nothing. I just had a tickle in my throat,' I say.

She steps closer to the table and looks down at me. Eyes too big for her small face, her slim frame squeezed uncomfortably into a too-short skirt and a too-low top. If it weren't for her clothes and that ugly silver stud through her bottom lip, she could be pretty. But all I see in front of me is the girl who's dating my boyfriend, the 'distraction' who's stopping him from getting back together with me.

I was lying to everyone when I said I didn't care. Of course I care. Rhys was the only good thing in my life and now that's gone. He didn't care about the small petty things that I used to torture myself about – how much I had to eat that day, how dull my skin looked, that stain on my favourite pink skirt. He didn't even care if I had make-up on. He said he liked me better without 'that gunk' on my face. He liked me for me, and that wasn't something that I was used to.

We got together purely out of convenience at first. We shared the same friends, went to the same parties, we were even in the same house at school. We participated in the same sports, of course Keith House always won at the school games. We were a team. And it was a team that I grew to love, and to need.

I don't even know when it started to go wrong, when he started to get bored. Because that's what happens, right? All boys get bored eventually. Or maybe they just get bored of *me*.

I called him so many times after but all he said was, 'You've changed, Luce.' Of course I've changed. I'm supposed to change. We all are. It's more that I've changed into someone he's no longer interested in.

It's funny really, because that's what my dad said to my mum before he left: 'You've changed, Julia.' I don't know if I ever told Rhys that.

Maybe we haven't changed. Maybe they have.

Now, I hardly ever see Dad.

He has a new family – young pretty blonde wife who used to work at the doctor's surgery, with a one-year-old on her hip. One year old. He left us fifteen months ago. The maths doesn't fit. He knows that. So when that woman walked around with a swollen belly, my dad sat at the dining table with us eating his Sunday roasts and reading his newspapers.

Not anymore. Now Mum rarely cooks or leaves the house. I don't know when she last showered. She completely crumbled the moment Dad walked out. And I have to deal with it every day. But back then I had Rhys to help me deal. Now, I don't. Now, I'm all alone in this.

He understood. He knew both my parents. He'd seen them when they were together, when Dad was faking the love and pretending he was in his forever family. Rhys used to come over for Sunday lunch sometimes when his mum and dad went out to the golf club to meet their friends. He sat with us, laughed with us.

Sometimes when I'm alone in my bedroom, I think about just how much I've lost in the past year, how much I'm still losing. All that time, all that precious time I could be spending with my dad, with Rhys.

Amber.

That's her name. My soon-to-be stepmum. Who leaves their family for a woman called Amber? That's who's standing in front me now. Amber. Trina. They're both the same. Both want what isn't theirs.

She's standing here at my table in the cafeteria. Mollie, Lily and Cara are watching me, anticipating what I'm going to do next. Honestly, I don't know. I never know.

I just keep pushing the boundaries until someone says something, until someone finally loves me enough to notice. I can feel the anger, the frustration, bubbling so close to the surface. I uncross my legs and lean into the table further and stare back at her, tempting her to push my buttons.

Go on, Trina. Start it.

She eventually rolls her eyes and walks away, wildly swinging her bag over her shoulder, her skirt slightly hitching up at the back.

See?

Amber.

They're all Ambers.

ULANA

Those girls.

With their short skirts and heels. Crisp white shirts with the first two buttons undone. Flickers of lace bras during Gym. Edges of pink thongs peeking out from freshly ironed black school trousers.

Those girls.

I feel bad for those girls. They don't know any different. They see images on TV and in magazines and aspire to be just that, not casting any doubt on the images they're being sold. They want their hair longer – not creepy long though – shinier, straighter, curlier, blonder but not too blonde. They want to be taller but, of course, not taller than any boy, thinner but…actually, there's never too thin. They open a magazine and all they see are skinny girls becoming skinnier, and getting praise for it. I see those girls at lunch, conflicted with the daunting choices of calories. Some don't even eat. Some have just a piece of fruit then say they had a big breakfast. They sip on water. Too much sugar in juice. Too many calories in a smoothie. Too much fat in a hot chocolate. Black coffee works too.

Then they go to the girls' toilets straight after. Some throw up, others readjust their short skirts and unbuttoned shirts. Most reapply their make-up for the afternoon. Glossy pink pouts. Thick dark eyebrows. Rosy cheeks. Matte noses. Black spider leg eyelashes. Contoured facial bones shimmering in highlighter. They dot concealer under their eyes, hiding the wrinkles they don't have but always see when they look in the mirror.

I hope they do it for themselves, and not for others. That they're not just parts of a game, being played, manipulated, moved onto tiny coloured squares for the next position. If not, I feel sorry for those girls. But they probably feel sorry for me. They think that I don't belong here. That I'm different. That I'm not free, like them. They're not free, not if they dress and look that way for others, for boys.

I feel a small tug on my hijab and it yanks a kirby grip from my hair. It slides down a little. When I turn I see those girls walking away. They look back at me and laugh. It's not like this all the time. But when it happens, it's always the same.

'Terrorist.'

Some whisper it, while others say it loud enough so

I can hear and so can all those around me. I'd be lying if I said it didn't bother me, of course it does. But that's what they want. They want to see me angry, see me cry. But I won't because I'm not ashamed or embarrassed. I know I won't be any less Muslim if I take off the hijab, I'll still be me. But I want to wear it because it's a part of who I am, where I'm from, and what I believe in. So they should be the ones who are ashamed and embarrassed. My parents gave me a choice when we first moved here, and although I don't wear a face veil like some girls and women back home, I've kept the hijab. I remain devoted to my faith, to my family, and to myself.

In all but one way.

Some might say, the worst way.

Sometimes I wish I wasn't the only Muslim here at this school, that I had someone else my age to talk to. I have Sophia, I know. She's a good friend to me. But sometimes I wish I had someone who understood more about my background. Someone who, maybe, was also going through what I'm going through – so I could speak to them about it. But I don't have anyone like that. Surely my parents considered that I'd be the only Muslim high-school student in this small village. The nearest mosque is almost a forty-five minute bus ride away.

'Hey!' Aiden from my chemistry class starts to chase them down the hallway but I hold my arm out to block him, being careful not to touch him or for him to touch me.

'Don't bother,' I say, bending down to pick up my folder.

'I'll get it.' He gets down there first and scoops it up. 'Here.'

'Thanks.' But when my fingers latch on, he doesn't let go.

'You shouldn't let those girls get away with that.'

'It's fine. Really. Hardly ever happens.'

'Liar.' He smiles at me, and slowly I feel the muscles in my face soften.

I tug at the folder again. This time he releases it, but his fingers brush against mine. It startles me and I look back to see if anyone saw it. Around us, people move in all directions, some darting into classrooms, others hanging out in the hallway. No one is looking at us.

No one sees us.

No one sees *me*.

I take a deep breath and walk away.

When I look back, he's still standing there.

My shoulder skims the corner of the wall, then I'm in a new hallway and I don't see him anymore.

I'm not used to being at a mixed-gender school. Boys sitting beside girls in classes. The girls' changing room next door to the boys' changing room. Girls standing in front of or behind boys in the lunch queue. Boys eating with girls they barely know. Nobody else here thinks this is strange but me.

Room 17 is dark, having not been used for classes all day. It's stuffy so one of the students cracks open a window. Cool clean air seeps in from the gap and I take a deep breath. The room is full. Classmates sit on desks, in chairs, lean against bookshelves. No one will notice me here.

I stand by the door in the back. The door handle jabs into my spine a little but I stay. This is the perfect spot. This is my spot. I stand here every week.

Some people take notes, while others hide their phones under the desks and text their friends. I don't know why they come. Most won't be applying to university and some won't get in even if they do. I know why I come. Not because we're obligated to sign up to one of the many UCAS sessions held throughout the school week. And not because I don't know how to navigate the online system, or don't know what universities are looking for in applicants. My grades are impeccable and I will certainly obtain unconditional offers for all the universities that I apply to. I could probably teach this class. In the second week, the instructor spent an hour walking us through how to complete the first page of the application form – 'Personal Information'. I'm pretty confident we can all recall our full name, address, date of birth and a contact telephone number.

That's not why I come here.

I wait until the lights dim, then watch as the instructor struggles to bring up the first slide of his PowerPoint presentation. Perfect time to slip out. No one turns. Anyone who does see me leave will probably just assume I'm going to the toilet and not question it.

The hallway is already quiet, even though it's only been fifteen minutes since the last bell. Those girls are long gone now. They're probably shopping for a new eyeliner in Boots on the way home, or picking up the new *Glamour* or *InStyle* from WHSmith. Sometimes I dislike them. Other times, I envy them. I don't have that luxury of 'free time'. Between waking up and going to sleep, my day is mapped out for me. What I wouldn't give for one afternoon after school where I could stay out as late as I want, skip dinner with the family, skip my evening readings, skip everything. Maybe I could leave school early, fake a sore belly, and have hours to myself – hours to lose to nothing, to lose to everything. But time slips by me, never glancing back. Time bumps into me in the hallway, and sits too close to me in the cafeteria. Time sits behind me in class, and ticks against my wrist, reminding me that seconds are passing, but that they don't belong to me. They belong to everyone else. They belong to those girls.

Time.

When I reach the top of the hill, I look down at the

watch on my wrist and adjust the alarm. I have thirty-five minutes. A deep breath escapes my lips. A flutter in my belly. Heat in my cheeks.

Boys sitting beside girls.

Girls meeting boys.

I bite my lip, feel the pressure between the teeth build.

And then I see him, waiting for me on the hill. He turns. He sees me. Finally someone sees me.

Then there comes that smile.

TRINA

<u>Journal Entry 1: 05.09.2018</u>

I saw him again this afternoon outside the biology department. I'd been rushing back from having a quick smoke outside the chemistry labs and was on my way to the girls' toilets to brush my teeth before class, when I turned the corner and saw him. I always seem to see him there in that hallway, so much so that I find myself hanging around and waiting there sometimes in case he passes by. I never used to go down that hallway. It branches off to the Literature & Languages classrooms and since I'm not taking English or French this year there's no need for me to venture down that way. But I know he has German after lunch period so instead of using the toilets by the chemistry wing, I now intentionally walk an extra four minutes out of my way for a chance of bumping into him. Is that stalking? No…surely not? I'll Google that later.

Anyway, today he was leaning against the wall, slapping his right palm against the stone to a particular rhythm like he was hearing a song that no one else could hear but him, while he waited for Mr Fischer to open the classroom door. And when the door did finally open, right before he turned his back on me – again – I could have sworn he looked up at me. Just briefly. Just long enough for me to notice and take a snapshot in my mind of his eyes, his body language, his expression.

He was kind of happy to see me, but also not wanting to show that he was. Why the games?

I like him.

He likes me.

This is a pretty easy problem to solve, isn't it?? He's the smart one, not me, so why isn't he figuring this out? If he likes me as much as I like him then there's no need for these mind games. We shouldn't be avoiding each other or pretending that we're not happy to see each other at school, in the hallway, outside at lunch, in the car park, when in fact we're thrilled. He doesn't have to not let on. He doesn't have to pretend. Not with me.

We had an amazing summer together. We spent practically all of our free time hanging out. He acted like we were in a proper relationship, but now this? It's as if the summer never happened. But it did. I know it did, and so does he. How much longer am I supposed to wait for him?

We don't have all the time in the world to take this

slowly if this is what is happening. We only have one more year together. He graduates in June and will go off to somewhere else new and exciting no doubt, Edinburgh or London or somewhere, and go to a fancy university that I can't pronounce the name of let alone ever stand a chance of getting into myself. And even if I did stand a chance – in some crazy universe where I actually got good enough grades and had made Head Girl – I couldn't afford to go.

Tuition rates are insane. I know there's funding, but I likely wouldn't be eligible for it because it's probably 'merit-based', right? People with bad grades and even worse attendance don't get funded to go to uni to get more bad grades and skip more classes. No, the government would prefer to spend its money on students who will actually pass the course and graduate to get a job to contribute to society. Me – I'm a risk. No contribution to society so far. Except to the food and drink industry. I do frequent the newsagent down the street quite a bit to get cheap vodka for the weekend. Does that count? No probably not.

And then there's the books. A friend of mine in the year above went to Kelvin College this year to do her Access to Nursing and she's already spent so much on the textbooks. And that's just for her first semester! One book was apparently forty-five quid! She probably won't even read it. You know anything that costs forty-five pounds will have tiny writing, graphs no doubt, and not the kinds of glossy colourful photos I like to see in a book!

And the housing options suck – I could stay at home with Mum and commute by bus to the nearest uni, which Rhys probably wouldn't choose. Or I could get student accommodation and be subjected to one toilet between twenty people. I could live with my friend but she lives in a council flat and probably couldn't fit me in anyway. She's also got a ten-month-old that her mum looks after during the day sometimes…me and a crying baby under one roof?

No.

University is not for me. Besides, I wouldn't even be able to work out how to complete the first page of the UCAS application.

University – or 'Further Education' as the guidance counsellor calls it – is for people who:

1. Read William Shakespeare (and understand what the hell he's saying – is it even in English?)
2. Drink tea in the afternoons, especially if it comes with a scone and a porcelain jar of clotted cream, whatever that is. Is it just regular cream? What makes it clotted?
3. Write with a pen that has a fluffy thing on the top that sits on a spring and bounces side to side when you write with it

4. Post photos of themselves with their parents, usually on some expensive holiday abroad – and they actually look normal, and HAPPY!
5. Detail volunteer work experience at homes for the elderly and children's hospitals on their profile and define this experience as 'life changing'
6. Use the term 'extra-curricular activities' on their CVs. Actually, bigger point here – it's for people who have CVs!
7. Have a five-year-plan that includes getting married and buying a fancy breed dog
8. Make daily 'To Do' lists and probably tick off each item as it's accomplished with that annoying fluffy top bobbing to the side pen!
9. Colour-coordinate their school folders
10. Season-coordinate their wardrobe – although this one sounds tempting as I hate digging into the back of my drawers in the dead of winter and only finding summer shorts and sleeveless vests

I'll tell you who it's not for – and keep in mind, this list is where I fall in. It's not for people who:

1. Don't read Shakespeare, but who have just one book on their bookshelf that has the inside pages ripped out and a stash of cigarettes inside (Mum goes through random bouts of 'Ciggies are so

bad for you' moments and searches my bags and drawers to 'help me')
2. Drink vodka and red bull – occasionally vodka and lemonade if I want to sleep that night for more than three minutes
3. Write with a black sharpie pen – and only on the bathroom doors of the boys' toilets at school
4. List 'partying' and 'sleeping' on their activity list
5. Post photos of their mates falling down the stairs of O'Neill's on a Saturday night
6. Have a mum that works at a home for the elderly for minimum wage, bathing creepy old men, while snobby girls with gel manicures breeze in for their daily thirty minutes of 'Read to an Old Person and Feel Good About Myself After'
7. Actually know what CV stands for…

So, as I said, this is where I fall in. And I mean, <u>clearly</u> fall in. Like there's no mistake about that.

And as you've probably guessed – the first section is where Rhys is. Although hopefully not the part about the pen with the fluffy top…or the afternoon tea with scones…but probably everything else, mind you.

BUT that didn't seem to bother him over the summer, did it?

No actually, it was the total opposite. He seemed really into me over the summer. We even met up a couple of times the week before school started back. And now he's acting distant, and I heard he's even been talking to his ex Lucy again. I hate that girl. STUCK UP SNOB!!!!!!!!!!!

She thinks she's better than everyone else, and she's not. She got dumped by Rhys before school ended for the summer and then got upset when he and I got together. She threw a drink in my face at Euan's party and called me a slut. Nice. Yesterday, she called me the same thing in the middle of the cafeteria then pretended that she was just coughing. She's so immature. What did Rhys ever see in her? And her friends are just as bad. I think I'm dumb – but Mollie Bridges? She takes the…whatever that saying is. And Cara and Lily are basically mini Lucys. UGGGHHHHHHHH! I can't wait for Friday. This week is going to SUCK!!!!!!

SOPHIA

'Are you not eating today?' Ulana asks me.

I look down at my empty tray that perches lightly on the cold metal racks of the cafeteria island. Round white plates line the silver shelves in the middle. There are no healthy choices at Birchwood High School, except if you count the salads, which most people do. I don't. Most swim in a sea of oily dressings. 'No, I don't really see anything that looks good today. I guess I'm not really hungry.'

She's looking at me in a weird way.

'I had a big breakfast,' I quickly add.

She eventually nods and gets back to choosing between tomato pasta or a ham and cheese roll for lunch. She's the only girl at school that I know who doesn't talk about her weight, or know the number of calories in a KitKat, or even read those magazines that claim to have 'the secret for losing a dress size in a week'. Which they don't because no magazine can tell the public that if they actually want to lose a dress size in one week then they'd basically have to starve themselves for that whole week.

I would give anything to have Ulana's confidence, her self-assurance.

But maybe not her parents. Gone would be my quiet evenings with Steve alone in the house if I had her parents. No, I'd be sneaking out back to meet my boyfriend too.

She struggles to lift up her full tray, while mine rests lightly on my forearms. 'Where do you want to sit?'

My eyes skim the crowd, quickly locking onto Lucy McNeil and her friends in the centre of the cafeteria. 'Maybe not there.'

We shuffle to a table at the side, in the back, and plop our trays down. Streaks of ketchup and mustard left behind from the last occupants make my tummy flip.

'You're really not hungry?'

I shake my head and poke at the bruised apple on my tray. 'Told you. Big breakfast.' I glance over to Lucy's table, her tanned brown skin, shiny dark hair falling around her shoulders. Girls like that are just born that way, while we have to claw our way up or risk being mediocre and forgettable our whole lives. 'Looks like someone's enjoyed a holiday abroad.'

'Who?' asks Ulana as she digs into her plate with a fork a little too small for her fingers.

'Lucy McNeil. Look how tanned she is. So jealous.'

'Burned you mean,' she says. 'Anyone who intention-ally sits out in the sun is just burning their skin.'

I take a bite of my apple. The waxy skin tastes like shards of plastic in my mouth. I gaze down at Ulana's pasta. 'How is it?'

She shrugs and takes another mouthful, some flakes of Parmesan falling from her fork. 'It's not Italia Nostra, but it'll do.'

'I love that place.' Freshly ground garlic and rosemary seep out from under the kitchen door and float through the restaurant, occasionally out onto the street. Beautiful circles of brick-oven pizzas loaded with fresh basil and mozzarella that stretches for yards. Tubes of red pasta dotted with black pepper served in bowls that have yellow and blue swirls looping around the edges. I clutch my belly as a low gurgle moves through my body. 'Have you ever thought about sex?' I suddenly blurt out.

Ulana coughs on a piece of pasta and sets her fork down.

I slap her on the back. 'Sorry.'

She rubs her eyes, a few drops trickling down, and coughs up again. She clears her throat and turns her chair towards me a little. 'I wasn't expecting that.'

'I was just wondering, you know, you...Aiden...?'

'Sophia, have you met my parents?' she laughs. The smile suddenly fades from her face as she edges in closer to the table and leans on her tray with an elbow. 'It's hard enough for me to get my head around the fact I'm dating a boy outside of my religion, but that…' She shakes her head.

'That's a no, then?'

'No. Definitely not.' She slides her tray away from her body and drops her fork down onto the plastic bowl.

'But you've thought about it?'

She shrugs and turns away, looking out beyond our little circular table.

'You *have* thought about it, haven't you?'

She leans in, her mouth close to my ear. 'Of course. I'm seventeen.'

I smile and sit back in the chair.

'But thinking about it is much different to actually doing it,' she adds.

I open my mouth to say something but an arm pulls me backwards. 'Steve!' He laughs and drops to his knees beside my chair. Leaning in, his lips meet mine.

'Still here,' Ulana loudly states, tapping my arm.

'Sorry.' I take his hand in mine and squeeze it gently. 'Will you call me tonight?'

'Yep, I will.' He winks at me then rushes off to catch up with his friends who stand at the back, pointing at us, teasing us. He playfully nudges the tall one in the back, Rhys, as he passes him. I can't help it; I turn to watch Rhys' ex-girlfriend's expression. Lucy McNeil watches him pass then flicks her hair in that Lucy way, before turning back to her friends, her posse. Those who I'll never sit with, never talk to at a party, never text with. But that's OK. Because I have Steve and that's all that matters to me now.

Ulana takes a big gulp of her water bottle and watches him walk away, eyeing his every step. She quickly puts the bottle down, turning into me again. 'Just make sure you're not getting pressured into anything, OK? It's your body. Your choice. Don't let anyone make you feel like you can't say no.'

I fiddle with the stem of my apple core, pushing it back and forth until it eventually snaps and breaks free from the fruit. 'I know,' I shrug, tossing it into the empty tray. I momentarily shake the idea from my mind, then commence a conversation on tonight's biology assignment.

But by the time I get home from school, I'm still thinking about it.

IT.

And before I've even changed out of my uniform for the evening, I'm upstairs, on my bed, at my laptop. Fingers quickly tapping at the black keys, and suddenly perfectly thin models with big bouncy hair and pouty lips stare back at me, all swathed in lace, chiffon and silk. My temples start to throb as dilemmas between 'Brazilians' and 'cheekies' and 'babydolls' and 'chemises' fill and overload my brain. Padded or push-up? Plunge or demi?

And what's a 'merrywidow'? It sounds like a character from a Marvel movie.

The bedroom swings open and my mum stands in the doorway, cleaning her hands with a mint-green tea towel. 'I didn't even hear you come in. Why didn't you say hi?'

'I thought you were at Aunt Bridget's this afternoon?' My swallow burns my throat.

'I was but I wanted to get a start on dinner. Your dad's finishing work early today. Quiet day at the office, I guess. I'm making a roast tonight. That OK?'

'But it's not Sunday?' We like to stick to traditions in our family, although the images in front of me are far from traditional. Is that a thong-filled Christmas tree bauble?

'Your father and I are going to the golf club this Sunday with his work friends.'

There was a time when Mum and Dad used to go there with Lucy's parents. It's funny that our parents were friends but we never were. Not even something like that brought us together. We were completely different people. Always will be. I bet she'd know what a 'merrywidow' is. She probably has one in black. Or maybe in red.

'Not going with the McNeils?'

'Oh no. We haven't seen them in a while. I think it's been about a year.'

'Really?'

'I did reach out a few times to invite them, but Julia

never got back to me. I don't even see her in town much anymore.'

'Oh, weird.' My fingers slowly reach for the laptop screen and I start to lower it half an inch at a time.

She stands at the door, still rubbing her hands. How can they not be dry by now?

'What are you up to, honey?'

A crisp silence hangs heavy in the hair. My palms start to get clammy. I feel like I might throw up on my MacBook at any second. 'Hmm?'

'Honey?' she asks again, her eyes burning through to the back of my skull.

I can't lie. I never could. I tried once or twice, but it was like she knew, like she could smell the deceit and dishonesty on my skin like cheap perfume.

'Um…a biology project,' I croak out, my voice a little too high at the end.

'What on?'

Oh. She wants details.

Think of something.

Think of something.

'Human anatomy,' I finally say, nodding my head.

'Oh, well I'm afraid I can't help you there. I never did know much about the human body.' Then she turns and leaves, closing the bedroom door tight behind her.

LUCY

I remember the day my dad left.

Branches creaking, slight bounce in the back door that hadn't been closed properly, it was a windy day. It howled and moaned, and dragged through our town like a rake in weeds, surfacing the weak roots in the soil. That was us that day. A weak root.

I hadn't always thought that. I'd thought we were a strong unit. That the three of us were a family, unbreakable to the core. We'd been happy. We watched films in the evenings during the week when I wasn't allowed to go out with my friends or Rhys. The weekends were mostly our own. Mum and Dad went to the golf club with the Greers, while I went to the cinema with Rhys or occasionally drank cheap white wine from a cardboard box and gossiped with Lily, Cara and Mollie about the hideous outfits people wore to high-school parties. Short skirts, tied-up tops, low-cut necklines, bright-coloured tights, sequins that sparkled a little too much, fake leather skirts that were more fake than leather. But during the week, where homework, early bedtimes and nutritionally dense dinners took precedence, my time was *our* time. Family time. We always ate at the dinner table – TV off, phones on silent. We talked about our day, our weekend plans, things that were bugging us. I talked and they listened. Now I talk and no one hears me. Mum's in a place that I can't reach, and never will, and Dad's 'busy'. He says that a lot now. 'Sorry, Luce. I've just been busy at work…Sorry, Luce, I can't this weekend. We're just so busy with the baby…' *Sorry. Sorry. Sorry.* Everyone is just so sorry, but nothing changes. Not even my memory of that night changes. I replay it sometimes. It makes me stronger.

I think.

My parents had been up all night – talking, arguing, crying. I don't know. I wasn't there in their bedroom. But I heard them. They never made me a part of the discussion or even considered me when making a decision. My dad had been late from work the evening before and his dinner had sat cold on the kitchen table for almost two hours before he walked in, navy coat strewn over his arm. They'd bickered about why he was always late from work, and my mum walked out of the living room. The bedroom door slammed upstairs and my dad had plopped down on the sofa beside me. I'd been texting

Rhys so my phone had been in my hand. I remember that because after my dad said what he did, I'd dropped the phone and it'd hit my foot.

He'd wrapped his arm around me, his fingers lightly resting on my upper arm. His voice was different, gravelly like he had a cold. He asked me how my day at school had been, and I told him about our social studies assignment and how I'd practised for the dance society's next performance at the arts centre on the high street, which of course I'd got the lead for. But when I asked him how his day had been, his face turned pale and he looked like he was going to cry. He didn't respond to my question, instead he coughed gently and turned his gaze to the yellow shaggy rug that I often lay my belly on while I finished my homework for the evening. I don't do that anymore. I don't do a lot of things that I used to.

He didn't look at me once while he said nine simple words. 'Everything is about to change. Please don't be scared.'

Change.

I didn't want anything to change. Why did it need to? We were doing just fine how we were. But it was no longer about us. There was suddenly someone new in this family. Another voice, one that hid from us in the shadows and slowly poisoned my dad's thoughts. One day there were three of us. Then the next, there were four. And soon, just two remained. The two left behind. The unwanted two.

That's why I hate Trina so much. Not because of what she wears, how she acts, what she says. But because all of a sudden she was just there. She became my Amber. And when Rhys ended it with me, saying we'd 'grown apart', all I thought about was how my mum must have felt being dumped, being tossed to the side for someone else. And I became angry. Really angry. And I started thinking about what people would say if they knew I'd been rejected by my dad and then by my boyfriend.

Before then I never had to think too much about what people thought of me. I didn't care. I did well at school, I had best friends, I had a boyfriend who treated me well, I was invested in after-school activities like the dance society and Amnesty UK. I was doing a good job at being me. Then one day Dad left the family and in a way, Mum left too. And I suddenly became aware of other people, and more importantly what they might think of me, be saying about me behind my back. What if they pitied me like the other 'children of divorces'? 'Poor Lucy has no dad anymore'... 'Aww, Lucy's dad left them...' Or worse, what if I became the topic of gossip? 'Did you hear, Lucy's dad walked out on her and her mum?...Did you know Lucy's parents are getting a divorce?...Guess what I found out this weekend?...'

I became consumed with what other people thought about me, terrified that they'd find out that my perfect life was all a lie, that my dad chose his new family over us, over me. That despite all the happy meals we shared together at that big oak table, all the movies we curled up on the sofa to watch with frozen banana chunks dipped in dark chocolate, that despite the holidays we went on every year where we took family selfies and posted them on social media, that fundamentally my dad was unhappy. That hurts me more. That he took into consideration all the years, all the memories, all the love, and still came to the conclusion that he'd be much happier with another wife and another child. That. Kills. Me.

So I decided that I wouldn't be the focus of hushed conversations, the words on scrunched up paper notes passed along in class under tables, the target of people's pointed fingers. And the only way to ensure that was to always be putting other people in that position. If I pointed the spotlight at others, no one could turn it on me. I'm not proud of who I became after my dad left, after Rhys left. But for now, it works. For now, I'll keep going and no one will find out my secrets. Never. But I'll keep finding out theirs.

ULANA

My fingers are red raw from rubbing. My nails ache from the pressure of pushing down. I think I chipped the middle nail because something sharp just rubbed against my thumb.

But I don't stop.

I get another paper towel from the girls' room dispenser and dampen it under the warm tap. Then I return to the stall door and continue scrubbing.

I know it's not my name or my reputation, but it could be. And if it was then I would hope that some girl would do me the same favour, show me the same respect.

Trina Davis is a <u>SLUT</u>

I can't leave it here, not that.

Who would do this?

Girls that have no idea. They trash reputation and then move on to the next victim. What if that said my name?

I can't imagine. What would my parents think? What would my dad say? How would I ever be able to face them again?

My fingers shake and the moist towel drops to the floor. My belly churns, a warm sensation moving upwards through my body, snaking its way up to my throat. I swallow it down, take a deep breath and tell myself: *It's not my name and it's not happening to me. No one knows about us.*

I check my watch. I'm late. He'll be wondering where I am. I have another go at the door then flush the paper towel down the toilet.

Grabbing my book bag, I rush out and through the back door. Feet on dried brown leaves from the birch trees, hands on the trunks of pines, I reach the spot. It's the perfect place, sheltered from the wind, and more importantly, from the school.

He stands by the bench – our bench – then starts pacing in front of it. He checks his watch and runs his hand through his hair.

'Aiden!'

He spins round, a wide smile stretching across his face. That smile. *My* smile.

I still remember the day I noticed Aiden for the first time. He'd been sitting in chemistry, one row in front of me, on the right. A PowerPoint presentation outlined the major components of atomic bonding and all around me people took frantic notes, our hands not able to keep up with the rapidly changing slides. My right hand was cramping and I rubbed, massaging into the muscle. It was at this time that I came to two realisations. Firstly, that I didn't need to be taking this many notes because I already knew all this. And secondly, that the boy sitting in the row in front of me, to my right, wouldn't stop turning around to look at me.

At first, I thought he was just curious. I was in full dress, the fabrics bought with my parents in Morocco, but my Western-bought jeans and grey Converse trainers stuck out from the bottom. He was interested in me. That was it. So I entertained him. I turned my face to him to let him know that I knew that he was watching me. His cheeks reddened and he turned his head back to the projection screen quickly. I remember putting my hand up to my mouth to stifle the smile that suddenly and unexpectedly came. And when I regained my composure, I looked up and saw that he was staring again. But this time he was smiling too. Smiling at me. Tiny dimples in the corners of his smiles, eyes wide and even in the darkened room, they had a sparkle to them. I looked away. And when I looked back – and I told myself not to so many times – the smile had been replaced by a goofy face. Half the class turned to face me as a loud giggle escaped my throat. Sophia had observed the interaction and I couldn't hide from the questions and playful elbows that followed in the days and weeks after. Every time he passed me in the hallway or smiled at me in class, she'd be there beaming from ear to ear, thrilled that for once in my life, I was doing something that wasn't on my 'Life Plan'. Instead I was doing something that should never be mixed with education and future life decisions – I was having fun.

It was innocent at first. Smiles, nods, innocent facial exchanges. Then it moved to verbal interactions where he'd ask me the time even though I saw the watch sticking out from his sleeve. He asked me about Morocco and I asked him about, well, everything – music, films, books. I was interested in every word that came out of his mouth. I was curious about what he liked, what he did with his time, and about those dimples. He made me laugh. He was funny, smart. He stood out from the others. He sought to be different. It wasn't an embarrassment for him but a requirement. He had an active desire to be so. And for the first time since we'd arrived in this country, he made me feel at home, a part of something outside of my obligations at school and at home.

It had almost ended before it had even started. He'd asked me out at the end of class, just to see a film at the cinema. But for me, that moment made me see that by just talking to him, I was crossing a line that I wouldn't be able to return to. That I was stepping away from my religion and my beliefs, and possibly abusing the trust of my parents. And that I was leading on a boy that I really, really liked. I knew we could never even be friends, not with how I was feeling towards him, let alone anything more. So I said no. I tried to explain to him why I was saying no, and he understood. And then we didn't talk for weeks after that. Those were the longest weeks of my life. The worst weeks. Week after week of regret, envy, anger, frustration, and something else, something much bigger.

Desire.

I still feel that now when I see him standing here.

I rush the next couple of steps and stagger into his arms. I hug him like I haven't seen him for weeks, even though we stood in this spot only two days ago.

'You're late. I thought you weren't coming?'

'Sorry, I got held up.' We sit, hands and fingers locked together as we usually do, and face the school.

'How was UCAS prep?'

'Very funny. Even just fifteen minutes of that is torture,' I laugh.

'Learning anything in yours? In mine, I learned how to bullet-point my skill set.' He smiles. 'But I think that's more for people who actually have a set of skills as opposed to me.'

I nudge him in the ribs with my elbow then lean my head on his shoulder.

Maybe no one will see us. Maybe we can keep on pretending as if this bubble that surrounds us now will stay just that and nothing can pop it. But I feel eyes on me all the time. I don't know how much longer I can keep all this up. I search for my father every second of the day, for my mother, for my neighbours, for my teachers, for those who'd use this information against me. People like Lucy McNeil, maybe even Steve who seems to hate me. He thinks I put 'rubbish' in Sophia's ear. I only tell her the truth. One day I hope she'll listen to me. I hope she'll trust what I tell her about him. But I also fear him too, and what he might say if I upset him too much. All those people wait for me to screw up, yet I've done my best to avoid them so far. But how much longer can I? When will I see them, or them me?

'Are you OK?' he finally asks, wrapping his arm around me.

I snuggle in closer, the wind breaking through my thin jacket.

'I don't know how much longer we can do this,' I say quietly.

'I know. It's getting colder. We have to find somewhere a little warmer to meet.'

That wasn't what I meant but I don't bring it up again. Maybe I'm enjoying living in this bubble too much. I turn to him and find warmth in his lips, in his arms.

Then I lean my head on his chest. I can't feel his heart

through his navy jumper, but I know it's beating under there. He wriggles underneath me.

'Are you uncomfortable?' I shift my weight to one hip, away from him to give him a little space.

'No, it's not that. I'm just getting…' He pulls a small wrapped gift from inside his pocket. It's box-shaped but the corners are squashed, caving in slightly. He tries to pop out the edges then gives up and drops the box into my hand. 'Happy six-month anniversary.'

I quickly sit up. 'Six months? It's really been that long?'

'You forgot?'

'No, I didn't forget…I just didn't exactly remember.' I smile, kissing him on the cheek.

He laughs and gestures towards my flat palm. 'Open it.'

My fingers clumsily unfold the gold tissue paper away from the sellotape. Inside is a small black cardboard box. Tugging the top away, the lid pops open. I gently pull out a thin braided turquoise band with a small silver heart looped through. 'Aiden…' The heart dangles down, shimmering a little as the light trickles in through the birch trees and strikes the silver.

He takes the bracelet and loops it over my wrist, struggling to fasten it. 'I think my fingers are too big for this,' he laughs. 'There, got it.'

My finger grazes my wrist, the braided ribbon soft under my touch, the heart pendant cold on my fingertip. 'It's beautiful. Thank you.'

It is beautiful. But that wasn't my first thought. I won't tell him that I worry what my parents will say when they find this bracelet in my room, in my bag, or on my wrist. It's just one more secret to hide, one more lie to tell.

After we say goodbye, it's the same routine as usual. I travel through the school, by the drama department, past the library. 'Sophia?'

She turns towards my direction and then a huge smile stretches up to her cheeks. 'Oh, hey.' She balances a pink-rimmed water bottle on top of a small stack of books, each with faded barcode labels facing out.

'Need a hand?' I say, reaching up and sliding off her glass water bottle.

'Thanks. That's my third one this year. I always seem to lose one in Steve's car and he never gives them back,' she giggles.

'What's all this for?' I nod towards the books. *Anatomy of the Human Body* sits at the top, a very graphic image of the female reproductive system staring at me intensely. 'Some light reading for biology?'

She clears her throat and squints her eyes. 'Oh, I just wanted to get a better understanding of…of, um…the human circulatory system.' Her eyes skim the floor by the feet and I can't help but smile. Her cheeks start to flush red and I put a hand to my mouth to stop myself laughing.

'Yeah, sure,' I grin. 'Come on, do you want to get a coffee on the walk home?'

She takes a deep breath and wrinkles up her nose like she's in pain. I've embarrassed her, I think. She nods and turns with me.

'What else are you working on?'

'I have a history paper due next week and then my French practice exam the week after.'

'I can help you with your French exam if you want?'

'You're so lucky. I wish I spoke it fluently.'

'You're good, really. You'll be fluent in no time.'

'Steve wants to take me to Paris after graduation.' She beams, pushing the door open with her hip. A coolness washes over us. The fabrics of my hijab billow out around me in the wind, while strands of Sophia's hair dance in the air, like she's floating in water.

'Jo's?'

'Hmm?' I say, my eyes still fixed on her shimmering long hair that's bobbing up and down on her back now.

'Jo's for coffee?'

I nod and follow her down the path through the courtyard. At the end is Birchwood Road, the street that connects the high school to the primary school and to the main town centre. There's not much to the centre itself: some shops, three hairdressers (why does a small town need more than one?), two florists, two bakeries, seven pubs (again, why does this town need that many?). But stationed in the middle of the town's library car park is a large red double-decker bus. Inside, the seats have been lifted and replaced with wooden benches, with feet that curl up like the letter S. At the front, where the driver should be, is a large white counter with a chalkboard sign that lists every kind of coffee and dairy-free alternative that, I truly believe, has ever been created. Jo's BusStop is our usual place, everyone's really. It's the only place to get 'vegan coffee' in town. I didn't know that was a thing until this year. Apparently milk just isn't 'in' anymore. Dairy-free, gluten-free, meat-free…basically any diet that's free of one major food group is a trend over here.

Sophia bounds up the stairs of the bus. 'Hi Jo! A medium sugar-free extra-hot vanilla latte with coconut milk, please. To go. Please.' She struggles with her books and her wallet, and looks up at me. 'Why are you smiling?'

'I'm just picturing my mum and dad's face if I ever ordered that in front of them.'

'What? You don't get lattes in Morocco?'

'Not like that!'

Sophia hands over a fiver and wrestles with the change she gets in return.

'You forgot your gluten-free raspberry and white chocolate loaf. Want me to order it with my coffee?'

She shakes her head quickly and leans against the counter as the woman who we call Jo, who's hopefully actually called Jo. 'No, not today.'

'Why not?'

She shrugs and is handed a tall white takeaway cup with a brown cardboard sleeve to keep her hands cool. She shifts to the side and lets me order. 'Coffee, please. Medium.'

Maybe-Jo stares at me for a moment, waiting for me to speak again. Finally, she does it for me. 'What kind of coffee?'

'Normal. No fancy milks or sugar-free syrups. Just a regular black coffee, please.'

Maybe-Jo rolls her eyes, as if my order is even more pretentious than Sophia's and turns to slide a glass coffee pot off the heat base. She pours the scalding dark chocolate brown liquid into a cup and hands it to me. 'Ninety pence, please.'

'Wait, why is yours so much cheaper than mine?' pouts Sophia, looking at her scattered silver coins in the palm of her hand.

'Why do you think?' I laugh, gesturing to her cup. 'You sure you don't want that raspberry loaf? I'll split it with you if you don't want to eat the whole thing?'

'Nah, thanks though.' She bounces off the step and stands outside the bus while I sprinkle some white sugar into my black coffee.

My feet land beside hers soon after and we start walking back through town. Instead of going straight up the street, back to school, we turn left down Abbot's Alley and spill out onto the car park at Aldi's. Then we cross over and take the river path back towards Golfview Road. Sophia lives in a slightly nicer neighbourhood than me. Her dad's a doctor like mine, but when we moved my dad's medical qualifications didn't meet British standards so he's the manager at Waitrose now. I know he misses medicine. A lot. But he'd never say it. For him, his sacrifices have granted me the kinds of opportunities I'd never have got back in Morocco. After Birchwood High School, a degree from a British university will get me a job anywhere. I'll never have to make the sacrifices that my dad made.

'I think I might switch to skimmed milk next time,' Sophia says, pulling my thoughts back to her, back to the river we walk beside, back to the life I've been afforded here.

'Oh, why? I thought you were vegan?'

'Skimmed milk has less calories than coconut milk.'

'Sophia, you don't need to be worrying about that. Ever. You're beautiful just the way you are.'

She scoffs and takes a sip of her coffee. She doesn't hear me. She's not listening. She's not seeing what I'm seeing. And I see skinny. I see skinny everywhere here.

I shake my head. One day she'll listen, she'll see. I just need to keep telling her until she does. A deep sigh escapes my lips. 'Just don't be one of "those girls", OK?'

'OK.' She laughs and takes another sip of her sugar-free, extra-hot, vegan…whatever.

***

53

Beyond the woods behind the school, up the dog-walkers' path, past the cyclists' trail, is a large open meadow surrounded by the trees that cocoon Birchwood High School. Around the end of April, buttercups the colour of an afternoon sun bloom and cover the entire meadow like a soft yellow blanket. It's around this time that I watch my school friends carry up a blanket and textbooks and spend their free study period basking in the mild sunshine. Outside of this time, the meadow is peaceful, empty of anyone else, like today. The only dents on the meadow ground are those made by Aiden and I as we lie on our backs, our heads touching.

It's a welcome break from the usual bench we meet at, and here we get to do something even more risky than sitting side by side. Not only do we hold hands, our touch hidden by the overgrown grass around us, but here we get to lie near each other. Here, our heads, our hands, our bodies touch. Here, we're closer than ever before. Here, we risk everything.

'What are you thinking about?' he asks me, as he shuffles in closer.

I push my shoulder gently into his and close the gap between us just a little more. 'I'm just thinking about Sophia. I don't know what it is, there's just something about Steve that I don't trust. And she seems different when she's with him.'

'How so?' he asks, as he turns and delicately places a

kiss on my shoulder, which is covered in dark fabric as it always is. But I imagine what his kiss would feel like and feel the insides of my stomach churn.

'Not as confident. I'm just worried that he'll hurt her.'

'You're a good friend,' he says.

I turn and bury my face into his shoulder. 'I hope so. Thank you.'

A slow whizzing of a motorbike somewhere beyond the meadow pulls my eyes to the bottom left of the field. And then I see something. A flutter of branches. A movement among the trees.

'What is it?' he asks, raising his hand to my back as I suddenly sit upright.

'I thought I saw something.' I strain my eyes and look deeper into the trees, but all I see are branches and leaves beginning to turn colour and wilt. 'I was so sure—'

'Don't worry. No one comes out here at this time. You might see a dog walker or cyclist, but that's about it.'

'That might be enough,' I mutter, staring into the trees again.

'Lie back down,' he urges. 'It's so peaceful here.'

I unfold my spine onto the meadow ground again, pressing each vertebra into the soft grass blanket until I flatten out, like Aiden beside me. 'Yeah, it's nice to be off that bench,' I laugh. Plucking a daisy from the ground, I hold it up to my nose and pretend it has a strong smell, like a peony.

'What kinds of flowers do you get at home?'

'In Morocco?'

'Yeah.'

I think back to the tree-lined streets and courtyard displays. Rows of oleander and hibiscus dotted alongside colourful tiled walls and marbled fountains. And for a moment, I'm back there. I'm back home. And everything seems distant, cold. I feel suddenly separated from my life here, from my time with Aiden. A cold shiver creeps up my spine and I sit up again, letting it escape from my body, float into the chilly air and get carried off to somewhere far from us.

'I don't remember,' I lie. Because the truth – the memories – just brings back that gap between us. That gap I don't like to remember.

'I'll have to Google it.'

'Hmm,' I mumble, closing my eyes and pushing the hot pink bougainvillea and date palms from my mind.

'Have you seen the buttercups grow here?'

I smile, open my eyes and stretch my fingers out wide as if I can feel the short stems of the creamy yellow flowers in my grasp already. Now I'm back here in this meadow, right now, with Aiden. The gap is a little smaller again. 'Yeah, they're really pretty. I love the yellow.'

'Your favourite colour.'

'Good memory.'

He sits up and turns onto his elbow, propping his

head with his hand. 'We can take a walk here when they bloom. Maybe have a picnic?'

'Can't. Too many people.'

'Oh.' He lies back down and looks up towards the sky, at a low-flying plane soaring and leaving a cloudy streak behind it. There's an RAF station nearby so occasionally you can see one of the training vessels overhead. He traces the cloudy line with his finger. 'We could take a walk somewhere else then?'

'Sure, maybe right in the middle of town. Maybe on my street.'

'I'm being serious.'

I turn until I'm now on my side and lean slightly more into him. 'You are?'

'Obviously not here. But how about we get the bus into Carron or Lennoxtown? That's about half an hour from here. We shouldn't see anyone there?'

'But what if we do?'

'We won't. We could walk around, see a movie—'

'Like a real date?' The words linger in my mouth and I hungrily grab at them, wanting to pull them close and devour them. A date. With my boyfriend. In public. For once, I'd feel normal, not different. For once, I could act like a typical seventeen-year-old teenager. I could act like one of those girls with time to waste, those I both envy and hate too.

'Imagine.' He smiles, gripping my hand.

'I already can. But it's so risky.'

'No, I really don't think so. I think it's genius.' A wide boyish grin stretches across his face, and I can't help but return it with one of my own.

'And when would we enact this genius plan of yours? It's riskier at the weekend.'

'So, a weekday?'

'How? We're at school!'

'You have a free period after lunch on Wednesdays.'

'And you have class.'

'So I'll miss it for once.'

I roll my eyes. Skipping class would never be an option for me, unless I was really sick. And I mean, *really* sick.

'We'll get the bus when the lunch bell rings at 11.35 and be back for the usual time UCAS Prep finishes. We'd have five hours together.'

'What if someone sees us getting on the bus?'

'They won't. And to be safe, we'll queue up separately and even sit apart.' He shimmies closer to me. 'Whatever it takes. Ulana. It'd be so nice to spend time with you off school grounds.'

His hand grips mine, tighter. I float my head back and see another RAF plane overhead. In the sky, no destination, no purpose. 'OK,' I say finally. 'Next Wednesday.'

'Next Wednesday,' he echoes.

'It's a—'

'—date,' he laughs. 'See, finishing each other's sentences.'

I nudge him playfully, then tuck my legs up underneath me.

'No,' he moans rolling back on the ground. 'Is it time already? Please say no.'

'Don't worry, this time next week we'll have five hours. We can suffer through our usual hour today.' I stretch my hand out and pull him up to standing. He holds his arms out wide and I collapse into them until I can feel his heartbeat against my right cheek.

TRINA

<u>Journal Entry 2: 14.09.2018</u>

I'm not sure when it was that Lucy and I started hating each other. We've always been polar opposites. Style, sense of humour (I have one!), social circles, academic interests (I have none!), financial situation (I'm also lacking in that area), family...

Everything from how we style our hair to what we eat for breakfast to what we think is a priority in our lives couldn't be further apart from the other's. But I can't really blame our long-standing feud on our differences. No, I think what we share is just a mutual dislike for one other, to the core. The deeeeeeeep core.

Which is funny because we were in most of the same classes at the beginning when we started Birchwood High School. Yes, she attended more classes than me overall, but there were times – a lot of times – we sat next to each other in class. I remember one particular English class that I'd forgotten my copy of *Little Women* and she shifted her chair closer to mine and let me read off her book. I didn't even have to ask her, she just did it. And when my mind wandered, which was often, she pointed to the sentence that we were meant to be following along with, pressing into the ink with her manicured rose-hued fingernail that was gently shaped into an oval. We were different back then too but we didn't hate each other. We weren't friends, we didn't eat lunch or even walk to the cafeteria together after the lunch bell rang, but if we saw each other in the hallway or in the girls' toilets, we either smiled and nodded, or said 'Hi' like we meant it. We did mean it, I think. She was different back then. She was friendly, she was nice to people. And she smiled a lot more.

Now she's an empty shell – plastic on the outside, hollow on the inside. Like one of those dolls that fit inside other dolls, you know the little one goes into the medium one which fits into the larger one and so on? That's perhaps not the best analogy or maybe doesn't even make sense, but I can't think of another one right now. If I do, I'll write it down later. Then I'll remember it for the next time I try to analyse Lucy's inner workings, which may take five seconds or five years. I don't know why she's so mean to everyone now. It's like she gets off on making people miserable, highlighting their flaws or their mistakes. It's like she looks for people's secrets and exposes them purely for some evil enjoyment. Nothing stays hidden around Lucy McNeil. All you can hope for at Birchwood is a smooth-sailing school year of living under her radar. If not, good luck. Because – You. Will. Need. It.

Lucy Freaking McNeil.

Pretty, smart, popular, well-liked, with a perfect boy-friend (now a perfect ex-boyfriend...), perfect family unit. I envied her. I'd always wanted the perfect family. Both a mum and a dad. My mum is amazing. She's a strong woman and she does what she can to support us, I understand that. There's nothing more I can ask her to do. She's trying to do it all. And she is. But I can't help but wonder what it would have been like had Dad not left. It's been so long, I don't even remember him to be honest. I think he stuck around for the first year or two of my life but took off after that. Mum thinks he was working as a promoter in Ibiza for a while, but we don't really hear too much about him now. That was just hearsay from old mutual friends they once shared. But Mum doesn't even hear from them now. I remember I used to call one of them Uncle Rob. He'd bring over Liquorice Allsorts for me, and the odd bunch of yellow daffodils for Mum that I'm pretty sure he stole from the neighbour's garden. I think he was quite keen on Mum for a while. But I don't remember him much after that. I guess he got bored and left us too. Everyone leaves eventually, right? Nothing's really permanent.

I don't know too much about him, just a few details from things Mum has said, or things I've found. Once around my twelfth birthday I suddenly felt an urge to go up to the attic to see if I could find anything about my dad. I missed him more than usual that year. I always miss him on my birthdays, at Christmas, at Easter when Mum and I roll chocolate eggs down the hill at Kings Park and point out all the five-bedroom houses on Park Place that we'd live in if we won the lottery.

But I missed him more that year. I think because I started my period right before my twelfth birthday and suddenly I felt like I was a woman and that Dad had now officially missed my entire childhood. And I started to panic that he'd miss my adulthood as well, that he'd miss more of my growing up, especially at a time when I needed him the most. I was changing, and everything around me was too. I wasn't a child anymore, but I wasn't an adult quite yet either. A bit like now, I guess. I still don't know what to do with my life, and no one can give me those answers but my mum and dad, right? They can at least steer me in the right direction, maybe? I needed my dad more than ever that birthday. And he's gone. Still.

So I dragged the ladder up against the hatch, and climbed up. The door was stiff, probably hadn't been opened for a while, and when it opened inwards it swung back and hit the floor. Mum wasn't home yet from work, so I didn't worry about waking her up. When I climbed up, I had to push through a cobweb and watch a spindly amber-hued spider scurry away, forced to rehome.

The boxes were in no clear order with the most recent at the front, the older years packed tightly at the back. No, nothing like that. Not here at 57 Huntley Road. Some of the boxes weren't even sealed properly, or upright. My pyjama bottoms were covered in dust and attic dirt before I'd even sat down. I started going through the boxes, one at a time. Slowly at first, then faster. Every time I finished one, more appeared, multiplying faster than bacteria in a warm environment. I learned that in home economics during a food safety lesson two years ago. I liked home economics, although it sounds weird when I think about it – the economics of the home.

Box after box, and nothing. Until I hit the last six boxes and there it was. A large padded envelope filled with photos, letters, even a mix CD. His entire life – with us anyway – fit into one A4 envelope. I wonder if his new life – without us – would still fit, or if it would need more boxes than this entire attic. Did his life flourish without us? Were we dragging him down?

There weren't many photos and in a couple, his face had been scraped out by a sharp utensil, likely by Mum in the weeks after he'd left. I'd do the same. But at least I saw his face in some. It wasn't always clear – his head was turned away in some, others he was laughing and his face was all scrunched up. But I could tell that he'd had a beard back then, that he liked grey and navy clothes, that his hair was cut short, and that I had his smile.

I still have the mix CD. I haven't played it yet. I've hidden it in my bra drawer for five years now and still haven't brought myself to listen to it. I know it'll just be music. Songs that he liked, bands he listened to in the car. But I'm scared. What if there are some songs that I like? Bands that I also listen to? I want to be like him but I'm also terrified that I am like him. What if I'm like him in other ways too? What if not only do we have the same smile, the same taste in music, but the same fear of the future, of change? What if I start a family someday and then decide to abandon it, like him? What if I'm the one that changes, or worse, the one that can't change?

I missed him a lot that day.

I still miss him, even now after all these years.

It's weird to miss someone you don't remember, right?

How can you miss someone whose voice you've never heard, whose face you've never touched? How can you miss someone that you know nothing about? Does he like football? Does he still have a beard or does he prefer to shave every morning? Does he have an allergy to peanuts or shellfish or anything like that? What's his favourite colour? What does he do all day with his time? Is he married again? Hopefully not, because I think legally he's still married to Mum and I'm pretty sure it's a crime to get married twice.

Did he have more children? Do I have a half-brother or half-sister somewhere out there?

Does he think about me? At one point, did he ever want to have a relationship with me?

We could have written each other, sent postcards, talked on the phone, FaceTimed. Maybe if he was rich he could have flown me to Ibiza and I'd tell everyone at school that my dad works in the clubs in Ibiza and can get me in for free.

But I don't live in that fantasy. In reality, I have no idea where my dad is and no idea what he even looks like now.

No, I don't have the perfect life. Far from it.

SOPHIA

I stare at the reflection in the full-length mirror on my wardrobe wondering what exactly Steve would change about me if he could. I know if I asked him, he would say nothing. He would say I'm perfect as is. But I don't believe that. No one's perfect, certainly not me. I would change a hundred things about myself. But I would love to know what he would change. I just wish he'd be honest if I asked him. Would it be my nose? My finger grazes the bridge, feeling a slight bump. I would change my nose. Shave off the bone. Smooth it out. No curve. No bump. Would it be my chin? My dad always says the slight dimple in the centre was 'cute'. But I don't want to be 'cute'. I'm sick of 'cute'.

I wish my eyes were bigger. Boys like big wide eyes on girls, lined with fluffy thick eyelashes slick with black mascara, rimmed with soft dark eyeliner. But there's nothing I can do about that. I can line them with as much mascara, eye pencil, shimmery shadow as possible, but there's no surgery to make eyes bigger. Or at least I don't think there is?

I turn to the side and take in my profile next. OK, my tummy is finally getting flatter. I've been cutting out starches, so no bread, pasta and rice. And definitely no to any sweets and crisps. I already feel so much better with myself. Even Ulana commented that I was looking thinner.

A ripped patchwork of magazine cutouts line the rectangular mirror. The ones I most aspire to look like are taped up at my eye level so I notice them more. The bottom is reserved for more fashion-based inspiration, or hair and make-up ideas.

I'd never thought about my body much at all before I met him. Everything was so much easier back then. I wouldn't do anything to change my relationship with him, to ever risk it, but I miss the innocence of that time, that confidence I had in myself because I didn't know about expectations and pressure. I didn't know there was one body we all had to have. No room for difference. We live in a factory where we're all built to look the same, be the same weight. And if the mould skips us, then it's our job to create it.

The perfect female body.

No excuses. We can all attain it. Anything else is just laziness. And I'm not lazy.

My eyes wander over to the shopping bags on the bed. Thin strips of lace and ribbon folded neatly in tight tissue paper secured with pink heart seals that I would have to split to open them. It was so nerve-wracking going into Boux Avenue after school today. I was terrified one of my mum's friends would be walking by, or worse, that someone from school would see me. Everyone would know why I was in there. I have a boyfriend, I'm seventeen, and I'm in a lingerie shop. Hmm, who wouldn't be able to guess the explosion of thoughts thrashing around in my mind right now?

I didn't know what size to get and I was too embarrassed to ask the shop assistant to measure me so I got a few different sizes and I'll just have to face going back in there to exchange them.

I try on the black Brazilian panty first, slipping my ankles through the very small leg gaps. Then I slide it up my legs and stand in front of the mirror. I longingly gaze at the soft cotton briefs on the bedroom floor that my mum bought me and sigh deeply. I guess those days of comfort are gone.

Next is the red chemise. But there are so many ribbons and straps, my limbs get tangled up. Arms flailing overhead, I try to pull the lace fabric over my head to start again, but the elasticated ribbon is looped around under my arm and over my neck and it's too tight. I feel like it's slicing into my skin.

I thrash about for a few seconds until I hear the front door bang.

My body is frozen in front of the mirror, right arm twisted up and back, left wrist caught in a ribbon. I just need to move my arm this way and—

'Sophia?' calls my mum from the bottom of the stairs.

No. Please no.

She's going to come up. She's going to find me like this. Then she'll know. And she'll try and stop me. She'll tell me I'm too young, too impressionable, that I should wait until I'm least forty years old and married to a respectable man. Probably a banker. Or an accountant.

'Sophia?'

It's worse if I don't answer her because then she might rush up the stairs and find me sooner.

'Hi Mum!' Too cheery. She'll pick up on that. I clear my throat and deepen my voice. 'I'm just changing from school. PE was really sweaty. I'll be downstairs soon.'

But she doesn't go away. I hear her footsteps on the stairs. Coming closer. One step at a time. And she's rabbiting on about a sale on coleslaw at Sainsbury's.

I rush over to the bed and with my free elbow drag the Boux Avenue purchases off onto the floor. Then I frantically kick them under the bed. The door starts to open so I run and slam my body against the wall behind the door. I stick my foot out and catch the door.

'Mum! I told you I was dressing. I'm completely naked!'

'Oh sorry, honey. I just wasn't sure if you could hear me—'

'Coleslaw. Sale. Yes, I heard you.'

This ribbon is cutting off my circulation. My body is tingling with pins and needles. I may have to cut myself out of this one and just suffer the thirty-pound cost.

'Do you want tea?'

Yes, give her a task to do. Downstairs. In the kitchen. At the other end of the house. Away from here.

'Yes, I would love tea! I'm so desperate for a cup of tea, Mum.'

She turns and starts down the stairs.

Thank. God.

I kick the door shut behind her and stagger over to the mirror. Twisting my elbow up, I yank it out from under the elasticated strap, likely dragging some skin with me, and then start on the ribbon that's slowly but certainly suffocating me.

When I'm finished, I stare at the red lacy near-death experience on my bedroom rug. Nodding confidently, I fold it up as neatly as possible and slide it back into the shopping bag, tag a little crushed but thankfully still attached. I'm all done with that one. No thanks.

I have time for one last try-on so I choose the one-piece body suit. Blue, like the colour of an early mid-morning sky. It slides on like a swimsuit, much easier than the lace contraption, and hugs close to my hips. While I stand in front of the mirror, deciding whether it's hugging a little close, my phone beeps from the bed. I know it's Steve because I set up his ringtone and text alerts to play 'Love' by Lana del Ray when it beeps.

I rush over and plop down on the bed. Huddling the phone close to my chest, to my heart, I open his text and immediately feel a big smile stretch tight across my face.

What are you up to?

Fingers trembling slightly, I curse auto-correct as my text comes out jumbled.

Noting much. Juice trying on sun clothes from Box Avenue :)

Stupid auto-correct! Now I sound like I'm drunk.

Sorry. Auto-correct! I'm just trying on something from Boux Avenue...

After what feels like a solid two minutes, he finally writes back.

Really?

Yep!

For me?

Maybe.

Can I see?

My mum is downstairs, so no! :)

Send me a photo?

I tip my head back so it lands softly on the pillow under me. A photo? A weird feeling settles into the bottom of stomach. I feel strange sending a photo of me like this out there into what…the 'Cloud'? Or is it called the 'iCloud'? Is that where it goes? And then what? I hear about hackers all the time who steal intimate photos of celebrities then post them on the internet. But I'm not a celebrity. And this is Steve. He'll make sure it's kept safe.

Promise you won't show your friends?
Promise.
And don't lose your phone!
Promise.

I slide off the bed and head back to the mirror. Phone raised, I start clicking, more than I need but I only want to send him the best. The ones where I look the prettiest and the thinnest. And definitely not 'cute'. I turn the camera around and start the selfie mode next, filling up my picture library.

Plopping down on the rug, I start scrolling through them, deleting most of them. I choose three and edit them as best I can – 'Enhance' to make the colour pop, 'Glamour' to soften the edges, 'Vintage' on the last one so it looks hazy and dreamlike. I exhaust all of the photo apps on my phone within minutes. My hands are getting clammy. Thumb hovering above the Send button, I take a deep breath.

It's just Steve. I know him. I trust him. I love him.
Send.

LUCY

'This year is going to be amazing,' I say, turning my hip towards Cara.

She nods in agreement, shifting the weight of her physics books from one arm to the other. 'I hope so. It's our last year. We have to make it epic. Do you think we'll still all be best friends when we're at uni?'

'Of course! Why wouldn't we be?' She's right. Once we go to university it'll all be different. People change, drift apart. My parents did. It's hard to predict if we'll still be friends by the end of this year, let alone at uni.

'Are you going to Lee's party on Saturday night?'

I push thoughts of the future from my mind. 'Definitely. What are you wearing?'

'I think my faded skinny jeans with that blue sequin top from H&M…what about you?'

'Well, I was going to wear my faded jeans and a black body suit with my rose Topshop bomber but it has sequins too so we'll look like twins.' I pucker my lips and scrunch up my nose, waiting for her response. She takes a few moments but then finally gets there.

'Oh, well you wear that and I'll just wear something else then?'

'Really?' I raise my eyebrows and feign surprise. 'You sure?'

She waves her hand casually and her books slide further down her hip. 'Yeah, it's fine.'

The classroom door opens before I can thank her and we all start rushing in, aiming for the same tables in the back row. No one wants to be in the first two rows with 'Mr I-Spit-When-I-Talk Anderson.' Last year, Mollie swore she caught a piece of his fish sandwich from lunch in her hair.

My feet get to the threshold then don't go any further. A warmness fills my insides and flows through my body, gathering into a knot in my belly. I grip onto the door-frame for balance.

'Are you coming in or what?' Cara asks, an unfamiliar expression spreading across her face.

I touch a cool palm to my burning cheek. 'Yeah, you go on in. I'm suddenly not feeling well.'

She shrugs and turns around, heading for the last table in the back row.

'Save me a seat!' I call after her as she disappears into a sea of bobbing heads.

My brown suede ballet pumps slap the tiled flooring as I get faster. Slamming into the door, I slide my bag off my shoulder until it drops heavily to the ground, probably cracking my phone screen, then hurry into the first cubicle. I barely have time to hold my hair back before hot bile rushes from my mouth into the toilet below.

There goes my tuna salad from lunch…and that macadamia nut cookie…wait, is that my porridge from this morning?

I rest my cheek on the toilet seat and groan loudly, hoping no one else is in here with me. Sitting back up, I rock forward until I'm squatting on my toes then slowly peel myself up to standing again. Flushing with my elbow – I don't do school germs – I wriggle out of the cubicle trying not to touch anything in the path to the sink. I splash cold water on my face, focusing more on the side of the cheek that was glued to the toilet seat. Leaning on the edge of the sink, I firmly plant a hand on each side.

I look rough. My pupils are bloodshot and my skin has a dull grey hue to its complexion. Must have been that tuna salad. I thought it tasted funny. I should have said something at the time. I'm probably not the only one who got sick after eating one. I straighten up and feel my back twinge. Now I feel like I need a massage. Maybe I'll ask Cara to go with me after school on Thursday to that Thai spa on the high street.

When I get back to physics, the attendance has already

been taken so I have to amble down the hall to the front office to correct the absence. My shoes flop weakly on the green and white floor as I round the corner. A tall familiar figure by the water fountain stops me.

He's wearing the grey and white striped T-shirt I bought him for Christmas with his white uniform shirt on top but unbuttoned. He always did push the rules to the very edge, not enough to warrant a write up, but just enough to get a couple of disapproving looks from the Assistant Head.

I quieten my footsteps and inch towards him. Leaning over him slightly, I clear my throat. 'Do you know how many germs are on that handle and maybe even on the dispenser itself. Didn't I teach you anything?'

Rhys jerks up and a half smile spreads slowly across his face. He's nervous, I can tell. I know him so well. His nostrils are flaring slightly as he's thinking of something funny but not too leading to say. His hands are flat against his thighs like he's thwarting the clamminess seeping in, and he's blinking a little faster than normal. I've studied that face for two years, not including the months before that when I first noticed him noticing me.

He clears his throat. 'Luce, what are you doing out of class?'

Luce.

I like it when he calls me that. It's a nickname that I'd avoided for years but when he started using it, I didn't mind so much. In fact, I grew to even love it. The way the 'L' sounds coils at the tip of his tongue before rolling down like a slide, ending with a hiss for the 'S.' Only he could make it quite so rhythmic. So harmonic.

'I missed attendance. You?'

'Just thirsty. Plus I needed to stretch my legs. Mrs Hamer is killing me.'

'Yeah, just wait until she gets to Jane Austen on the syllabus. She gets really fired up then.'

'She just reenacted the forest dance from *The Crucible*.' His face softens and his eyes stretch out into thin slits as he starts giggling.

I hear the familiar eruption from my lips as a laugh from deep down in my belly escapes my mouth. He always could make me laugh. Even when I was mad at him, which seemed to be more frequent nearer the end of last school year when Dad's new baby was born.

New baby = New family.

New life.

As if he remembers the past few months, he abruptly stops laughing and wedges his hands deep into his pockets. He rocks back slightly on his heels and when he lands, he bites down a little on his lip. 'How are you anyway?'

'I'm OK.' I hope he doesn't smell the vomit on my breath, although it's hard to look cute after such a display of illness in a school toilet.

'Did you see your dad much over the summer?'

I want to say, 'No, he doesn't have time for me any-more' but instead I shake my head, and loop some hair around my finger, twisting and coiling it into loose curls.

'I'm really sorry about the summer.'

'You didn't return my texts or call me.'

'I know. I just needed a little space.'

'Did Trina help you with that?' I resist putting a hand up to my mouth to feign regret, though I just couldn't help it. The words slipped so easily from my lips. A warm sensation builds in my stomach and I hope it's not bile again.

'Birchwood High loves its gossip,' he simply replies, leaving me with that warm feeling to spread up to my cheeks. Sickness again? Regret? Love? Or maybe that's irritation.

'So it's not true?'

'What?'

Is he trying to make me mad deliberately? Does he want me to explode right here in front of Mrs Hamer's terrible rendition of John Proctor's speech?

'Are you or aren't you seeing Trina Davis now?'

He moves his shoulders into what looks like an attempt at a casual shrug, but fails. 'I'm not sure. We're taking it slow.'

My belly hurts. I thought he'd deny it or brush it off as a casual summer fling, but not this. This sounds… serious. This sounds like he's over me.

I edge a little closer to his body and soften my voice. 'I missed you this summer.' I reach out to touch him but he rocks back on his heels, seemingly accidental but I know he's intentionally avoiding any physical contact with me.

Suddenly recalling the last ten minutes with my head in the toilet bowl, I take a step back away from him and tug at a loose strand of hair in front of my face, tucking it back into the section where it belongs – curled slightly but not enough to look like too much effort. Rhys liked the natural look.

'I just don't get it. You can do so much better than that girl.'

He shakes his head and smiles. 'You hate everyone, Luce.'

'No, just her.'

'Why?'

'She's such a slut. She's been with every guy at this school practically.'

'I think that's an exaggeration,' he says, running his hand through his hair.

I like it when he does that. But the fact he's sticking up for her is making that warm sensation turn into a scalding pit of fire.

'No, it's not! She looks like she gets dressed in the dark most days. Today I think I saw her tacky red thong sticking out from her waistband. I mean, come on Rhys! Seriously? You rebounded with her?'

His face tightens, any glimmer from his eyes quickly fading. 'I'd better get back to Hamer's class. And you should sort your attendance quick, before they log it in the system.'

He starts back to the classroom on the left, while I face the front office, the light from the outside streaming in and striking the tiles illuminating the green in the swirls. I know better, but I look back anyway.

He doesn't turn around to meet my gaze like he used to when we parted. No, not anymore. Now he just walks on. I'm the one who's standing there watching him leave.

By the time I return to physics, I've missed a short animation on kinetic energy and apparently Euan's fall from the high-top chair by the 3D model table. Cara's halfway through a mediocre sketch of Mr Anderson, not exactly of the highest quality from someone applying to Edinburgh University's fine art programme.

I'm going to be a doctor. My grades are perfect so the rest of Birchwood High School should be a breeze for me. I can concentrate on what's important – getting Rhys back. I miss him so much. The summer was torture for me. And while I cried over him, over my dad, he was getting 'space' with another girl. I loved him. I still do. I think.

I skip free period at the end of the day, having already completed and submitted my homework, and walk home early. I still feel icky after my puke session and I could do with some air.

It's light outside, autumn only just settling in. Pine trees erupt from the soil around me and stretch high in the sky, their leaves singed with coppery reds and amber oranges, drooping slightly from the stem. The foliage is nothing compared to Glen Affric though. We took a camping trip there when I was around eight or nine years old. Me, Mum and Dad. The way it used to be. Us three and no one else. We needed no one else at that point.

While Dad struggled with the tent Mum blew up the air mattresses with a battery-operated pump. After our 'home' was set up and secured to the ground we went for a stroll on the trails and cooked sausages over the portable grill. There were no smartphones at that time, no celebrity magazines to be engrossed in, no arguing between Mum and Dad, no Trinas, no Ambers, or new babies. Life back then was just so much simpler. Now it's a muddled mess of regret, insecurity and hate.

My feet crunch over the twigs and dried leaves as the trail through the woods narrows under the trees. I used to walk here with my dad when he was still around. We had a cocker spaniel called Jack which he took with him when he left. Strange. He took his dog and a suitcase of clothes, but not his daughter or any of the family photos. I wonder if Jack's even Jack still. Maybe he's a Rufus or a Harvey. Knowing what I do know about Amber, and that's minimal, Jack's probably Fluffy or Doodles, or something equally unimaginative.

My body starts to drag near the end of the trail, my house thankfully just beyond the gates. I'm so tired all the time now. All I want to do is sleep. When winter comes and darkness really creeps in and stays, it's going to be so hard to get up in the mornings for school. I used to be such an early bird, jumping out from the warm covers at the first chime of my alarm. Some days I didn't even need an alarm, my body just wanted to wake that early.

But not now. Now my mum has to knock on the door really obnoxiously loud and call my name at least three times. It would probably take her less time to just make me a cup of coffee in the morning and bring it to me, actually make herself useful for once. But I guess I should be grateful she's able to get herself out of bed a bit more these days. I got a glimpse this summer of how she must have felt when Dad left. The overwhelming loss, the gossip of a new girlfriend, the confusion, then the anger. I felt all that too. But I couldn't confide in her because she wasn't there. She was stuck up in her bedroom alternating between antidepressants and Merlot. Up. Down. Her moods are all over the place.

Shutting the back door behind me, I trudge up the stairs towards my bedroom. I drop my book bag by the door and collapse my body into the plush grey armchair in front of the dresser that Dad painted white for me so it would match the rest of my bedroom after I complained that mahogany in a room of white was torture for a self-proclaimed 'control freak' like me. I lean back into it and let the squishy fabric envelop my tired body and stare at the unfamiliar reflection. My face is even more grey now, almost the same shade as the armchair and my face is breaking out, which never happens unless it's my time of the month…wait, when is that actually? Soon. Must be.

I glance over my shoulder, eyes skimming the floor for my bag, where I keep my phone, a power bank in case it dies during school hours, which would be a complete nightmare, a MAC lip gloss, oil-blotting sheets, and what I'm looking for – my diary. I yank it out from the side pouch of the bag and flick through the pages until I go back to August where a star sits right under the 10th. It's only been a month and a half, that's not bad. Right? I had that spotting at the end of August so that probably counts too.

I just don't feel right. I don't feel like myself. Maybe I'm getting my period finally, or maybe…

Maybe…

No. That's ridiculous. I'm seventeen. That's impossible. Well, it's not impossible, it's just…no.

Oh.

My.

God.

84

ULANA

'So, there's been how many of the same movie?'

Aiden shakes his head, and lets out one of the cute exasperated laughs that he does when I ask him lots of questions about his favourite films. 'This is the fourth. Well, six if you count the Alien versus Predator movies,' he says.

'Six? Was this a prequel we just saw?'

'No, it's another sequel.'

'Are the others the same?'

'Pretty much, yeah.'

'So in all of them, alien hunters come to earth in a spaceship and kill people?'

'Basically, yeah.' He smiles.

'Sounds like they need new material if you ask me.' I'd stupidly agreed to let Aiden choose the movie, and although it was exciting to be in a public place with him, sitting side by side, legs touching, and sharing popcorn,

I'd spent the last two and half hours trying to decipher the premise of a seemingly very simple science-fiction movie. But I could have seen any movie with Aiden and I wouldn't have paid attention to it. All I thought about in that cinema was him.

As if he can read my mind he grabs my hand, squeezing it tight to his chest. He brings it up to his lips then places a gentle kiss on my hand, between the thumb and the index. A warm sensation builds inside me, and I lower my head so he doesn't see my beetroot face. 'I've had a lot of fun today.'

'Me too.'

'I was definitely a little anxious at first—'

'Really? I never would have guessed!'

'OK, maybe I was more than a little anxious. But you're right. There's so many people here, it's the middle of the day, during a week, no one knows us here.'

He squeezes my hand tighter. 'Does that mean we can do this again?'

I squeeze back. 'Definitely.'

We walk through the car park, up to the bus station, where yellow daffodils line the benches, standing tall against the incoming winter season. Yellow, like the buttercups back in the meadow. The meadow that I can't walk through with Aiden.

'So, I was thinking—'

'Did it hurt?'

'Funny.' He clears his throat. His shoulders bounce up and down. Is he nervous?

'I was thinking you could come over for Sunday lunch this weekend?'

'Where?'

'To my house.'

I slow my pace until my feet are no longer moving. 'To your house? Will your parents be there?'

'I would hope so. I can't cook a Sunday roast!' he laughs, but it's not real. It's his fake laugh. I know all his real laughs.

'You're asking me to meet your parents on Sunday?'

He starts rocking back and forth on his toes. 'I know, I know. But I promise you, they won't say a word of it to anyone—'

'What would I say to my parents?'

'Tell them you're going over to Sophia's for lunch or to study?'

'And what if they call Sophia's parents?'

'They would do that?'

'I don't know, Aiden! But they could! And I'm not willing to take the risk!'

'We took a risk today. A big risk. There's no risk involved on Sunday. Trust me, I've thought this through. No one will see us, no one will know.'

'A different town, a city over thirty minutes from our houses is fine. But a weekend, in the same town, in the same house? What if my dad offers to walk me to Sophia's house then he sees her parents? I can't expect them to lie for me too. This is getting out of hand—'

'What does that mean?'

'It means I should have never have come here with you today because now you think this is normal. This isn't normal, not for us. This is just becoming too risky.'

'So, what if it is? So what? Aren't we worth the risk?'

I shake my head and try to walk away but he gently touches my arm and turns me round towards him again.

'Aren't "we" worth the risk, Ulana?' he says again as he stands in front of me, looking at me, waiting. His question hangs dryly in the air, waiting for me to grab it, to grab him and reassure him. But I don't say anything. I don't what to say. The risk he talks about is just a word, an idea, merely a potential obstacle that may or may not arise in our – his – future. But that risk to me is everything. He doesn't know. He has no idea what it's like to feel torn between my beliefs and him, to feel like I have to choose between my religion and love.

'You just don't understand. You couldn't.' I grab at the edges of the bus and hoist myself onto the top step. I lay the return ticket on the driver's counter and walk to the back of the bus. Aiden follows me onto the bus but doesn't sit beside me. He doesn't sit anywhere near me. He heads up the stairs of the double decker and disappears somewhere above me. Away from me.

I wait for him off the bus, ready to say the words he wants to hear, but it's too late. He flops down the steps and marches past me as if I'm invisible, like I was to him before he finally noticed me.

I walk home slowly later that afternoon. I feel everything. The cold breeze on my cheeks. The damp moss on my fingertips. The vibrations from the passing cars on my eardrums. The wet mist on my nose. And when I get home, back to reality, I still think about our conversation. I think about it all that night.

It consumes my thoughts, my entire existence. While my dad asked about my chemistry assignment and my mum fussed over dinner and gossiped about the neighbour's daughter who staggered home, probably drunk, at midnight on Saturday night while her 'poor parents slept unaware in their beds', I replayed his words over and over again.

'Aren't "we" worth the risk, Ulana?'

Why didn't I say yes?

The next morning, I can't take it anymore. I risk everything, break all my rules, just to talk to him. I can't have him go through another minute thinking I don't care about him. I can't have another sleepless night having ended a conversation like that. We barely get time together as it is, so the little moments we do manage to pocket, we can't waste them. I don't have time to waste. It's not a luxury for me as it is for others.

I'll hover outside PE, talk to him for a few minutes while his class is preoccupied with bloody knees, callouses, dirty shorts and sweaty shirts. Maybe I'm just scared that he won't be there this afternoon in the woods. That maybe I'll sit on that bench, in the cold, and wait, just wasting time. And if he doesn't come today, I'll know. I'll know that the risks I took will have all been for nothing. But most of all, I'll know that if he doesn't come today, he may not come tomorrow or the day after. And I will have lost him, forever.

My face fills the window into the basketball court. My hands grip the ledge, getting clammier the longer I wait. Inside, clusters of girls play netball on the far right of the court, while a large crowd of boys circle around the coach on the left. I see Steve. I see Euan, Lee, Matt, Andrew, Ollie, that boy who blew up the bunsen burner in chemistry last year and singed his hair – all boys I shouldn't even know the names of, let alone be watching in their shorts that sit a little too high above the knee. But not Aiden. I don't see him anywhere.

Where is he? He should be in PE. He's always in PE at this time. But not today. Why not today?

Maybe he went home sick.

I scoop up my bag and rush to the front office. Mrs

MacIntyre greets me when I push open the glass door. 'Ulana, how can I help you?'

She's nice to me. Every Christmas my parents give her and every other staff member a small box of chocolates as a thank you. They're generous like that, thoughtful, respectful. And yet here I stand in front of her, about to lie to her, to my parents, to everyone. I have no respect.

'I was walking by PE and Mr Gerrard asked me to check on a student...um, I think it was Aiden McDonald?' My voice is a little too high, a bit on the shaky side. She knows. She must know. Maybe she'll even tell the headmaster, or call my parents, tell them that she has concerns, that she thinks I'm lying. Maybe they'll all start to dig into my after-school activities, find out that I've been leaving UCAS prep early. Maybe they'll find out where I've really been going, who I've really been meeting with.

But if she's suspicious, she doesn't let on. Instead, she slides over a manila folder and opens it. She runs her name down the page with a manicured index finger, tinted with a green shade. Green like the colour of the birch trees in the spring, the trees that our school is named after, the trees that Aiden and I meet under.

'He's not on my list. He didn't go home sick. Is he absent?'

'No, no. Perhaps he must have been still changing for

basketball. I'll let PE know,' I say. 'Thank you.' I turn and hurry out before she can ask me any questions.

I gaze up and down the hallway outside the office, pulling and looping the straps on my bag. Why is it when you urgently need to see someone, you can never find them?

TRINA

Why is it when you never want to see a person, all you do is see them?

Lucy is everywhere!

It's like she's stalking me, waiting around every corner, under every floorboard, behind doors. She's obsessed with me. She just won't let this past summer go. I'm sure she's finding it very difficult to process in her pea-sized brain that <u>her boyfriend chose me over her</u>. Ex-boyfriend might I add.

<u>EX</u>.

As in not together anymore, broken up, never getting back together. In my experience, and it's not like I've dated a lot of people (actually none except Rhys, if that's what we're doing), but I thought when two people break up both are free to date. I'm sure she moved on too over the summer, with lots of people likely, so why is she fixating on who Rhys is moving on with? Or maybe it's nothing to do with him. But it's all to do with me. She hates me. If Rhys had moved on with someone else, maybe she wouldn't have minded. But me? I didn't even know her before all this. I stayed out of her way, avoided her and her little minions whenever I could. Up until this summer, I'd never really thought about her, let alone said a bad word about her. She was just the pretty girl who shared a book with me in English two years ago, and someone I said 'Hi' to occasionally if we caught each other's eye in the hallway.

Yet she's going out of her way to bash me to everyone. She just loves to torture me at school. She shouts 'Slut' when I walk by then either looks away or pretends it was just a cough – is she five years old? And she deliberately nudges into me when we pass, sometimes with such force that it knocks me into the wall. Yesterday she intentionally threw the volleyball at my face then pretended that she was sorry by running over and fake-hugging me, while whispering in my ear: 'Maybe that bump will improve your face. You can thank me later.' Mr Simms even praised her for 'checking on me, making sure I was OK'. Unbelievable. That girl is a <u>professional</u> at what she does.

What she doesn't know – and this is quite funny – is that Rhys has been texting ME all week. Yes, he's been showering me with texts, one almost every day, asking how I am, talking about the summer we had together, he even wrote: 'I really enjoyed the summer with you. I didn't want it to end.'

'Didn't want it to end?' He may as well have said 'I Love You Trina'!!!

Of course, I've been texting him back. I tried playing it cool, but honestly, I really like him. I'm done with games with boys – leading them on, not responding to their texts, kissing them at the weekend but ignoring them come Monday. Rhys is more mature than that, and since I've met him I'm more mature. This sounds so clichéd but he really does make me a better person. And maybe he did that for Lucy and now that they're broken up she's gone back to being who she really is.

I can't wait for Lee's party this Saturday. I'm going to go and look amazing just so Rhys notices me and finally acknowledges me in public, in front of all of his friends (and maybe a little to mess with her!). I'll go shopping after school and pick up a new outfit from H&M – but leave the tags on of course because I can't afford to actually buy it. I'll return it all next week after I've aired it outside to get rid of any smoke smells. Hopefully someone won't spill their drink on me because then I really will be screwed. How do you explain that? 'Um, sorry, I was trying it on at home in my bedroom and I accidentally spilled my juice. Oh yes, it might smell of vodka and

Coke but really it's just Ribena' (while smiling sweetly and holding the receipt in my hand).

I might try something different with my make-up too? Maybe tone down the black eyeliner a little, try the more natural look? No, not for Rhys, because I refuse to change for anyone, but for me. I don't feel like I need so much make-up on anymore. My skin has cleared up a lot over the last year and when I look in the mirror I don't entirely hate the person I see staring back. Actually, I'm feeling pretty confident these days. I've never been one to care about weight, or obsess over what size I'm buying in Topshop, and maybe that's because I've never had an issue with my weight. I eat whatever I want.

Today I Ate:

- Breakfast: 2 chocolate frosted pop tarts and a milky coffee with 2 sugars
- Breaktime: a packet of salt and vinegar crisps, and 1 cigarette
- Lunch: a chip butty from the fish shop down the street, Coke and 1 cigarette ('borrowed' from Lee)
- After school: It's only 5.10 p.m. and I've already had a Pot Noodle (Did you know the Chicken & Mushroom has no chicken in it?? It's actually vegetarian! Vegan too, I think! Crazy, eh?!)

– Dinner: Not sure yet, whatever I can find in the freezer to stick in the oven for Mum and me but guaranteed there won't be veggies anywhere on our plates!

I always laugh at girls who pick at salads and fruit at lunchtime at school, thinking that if they get fat no boy will want them. Saying that, I know how shallow boys can be, so wouldn't put it past them.

Except for Rhys. Not Rhys. He doesn't care about that stuff. He's different :)

I just hope he doesn't believe all the rumours that go about school. And there's always rumours. Last year, Fisher told everyone that we had sex at Sara's party. No, we kissed and that was it. Believe me, that was enough! He tasted like the inside of a toilet! But he spread that rumour around and no doubt everyone believed him. Who cares? I don't. If telling lies about girls makes him feel like a man, then I pity him.

Besides, a month later he accidentally blew up the bunsen burner in his chemistry class and burned the front part of his hair! It was amazing! He had to shave his head, it was so bad!!!

<u>HAHAHAHA!</u>

He called me a slut in front of his friends when I laughed at him. Speaking of, someone wrote TRINA DAVIS IS A SLUT in the first-floor toilets again.

Really?

That's the best you can come up with, Lucy?

Very original. Assuming it's her anyway – who else would it be?

Not that I thought that much of her imaginative skills or overall intellect anyway. OK, fine girls like that always get into uni, and girls like me don't. Lucy ticks off about ninety per cent of that uni list.

Actually, let's see that list again:

<u>University – Further Education – is for people who:</u>

1. Read William Shakespeare – last May, Lucy demanded to play the lead in *Romeo and Juliet* in the end-of-year school play, and guess what? GOT it without even needing to audition

2. Drink tea in the afternoons, especially if it comes with a scone – OK, I can't prove this one, but I'm sure she does this

3. Write with a pen that has a fluffy thing on the top – if I have to see her pink and gold feather pen one more time, I'm going to rip the feather off and feed it to her!!

4. Post photos of their parents – and they actually look normal, and HAPPY! – oh look, right there on Facebook: Mummy, Daddy, Lucy, and little cute cocker spaniel Jack…Jack? I'm surprised she

didn't call him Fluffy or Doodles or something like that

5. Detail volunteer work experience at elderly homes and children's hospitals on their profile – tick

6. Use the term 'extra-curricular activities' on their CVs…for people who <u>have</u> CVs! – tick

7. Have a five-year-plan that includes getting married and buying a fancy breed dog – again, I can't literally prove this, but I'd bet my life on it. So I'm giving that a tick.

8. Make daily 'To Do' lists – she even has a 'To Do' List notepad with a fridge magnet attached!! She carries it around everywhere then sits it on the table in the Caf as if some miraculously intellectual thought will spring to mind mid-lunch and she'll just HAVE to write it down in case she (gasps!) forgets!

9. Colour-coordinate their school folders – seen this, TICK!

10. Season-coordinate their wardrobe – urgh!!! Triple tick!

But maybe at the end of the day, she'll be laughing at me. Because when school ends, she's out of here. She can pack her bags and skip off to uni anywhere in the world. And me? I'm stuck here. I can't leave Mum by herself. I'll get a proper full-time job and start helping her with the bills. The debt just keeps piling up, and she pretends as if it's not urgent right now but it is. The red letters on the envelopes tell me 'URGENT'.

But until real-life smacks me in the face, I'll enjoy being a teenager for a little longer. Until then, I'll continue being me, even if some girls at school think that writing 'Slut' on the toilet door will bring me down – because it won't.

I mean, yeah, of course it hurts a little. I don't want everyone thinking that, but it is what is. That's what my mum always says, 'Not everyone is going to love you, Trina. But it is what it is.'

I never used to be like this. I never used to care what girls at school thought of me or whether boys liked me. Yes, I enjoy wearing skirts a little shorter than the other girls, yes, I like low-cut tops and lace bras, but what bothers me is when people assume that I'm doing it to look good for a boy. I do it for me. I'm confident in myself, and if my confidence makes someone else jealous or question their own self-esteem, then sorry but I'm not going to change. This is who I am. I could never imagine pretending to be someone I'm not for a boy. I like Rhys <u>A LOT</u> but if he asked me to change, I'd tell him where to go. I'm not changing for anyone. I'm happy with who I am, and I will never be put down by any girl or any guy.

Speaking of, heard another rumour today (no surprises here though) that Steve cheated on Sophia Greer last weekend. I doubt it was the first time either. People like

Steve don't change. I do feel bad for Sophia though. She seems really nice. And I mean genuinely nice, not fake nice. Wish I'd got to know her more this year, especially since we're in study period at the same time. But as my mum says, 'it is what it is'. Maybe we still can get to know each other. It's only October. There's still time. She's good friends with Ulana. I wish I still was. Maybe I wouldn't have such a reputation at school had Ulana and I stayed friends. But people change, I guess, drift apart. That's what happened with us, I think. Or maybe she drifted away from me. I never found another friend like her after that. But then again, I've never really been the type of girl that has lots of girlfriends. I've always got on better with guys. Less drama. Less competition. Less…well, everything. Girls can be mean, girls gossip…

I still wish I had a close girlfriend though. Don't tell anyone I said that.

SOPHIA

'It's all my fault.'

'What?'

'It's all my fault,' I say again. When I look up, Ulana still stands there, hands on her hips. Waiting for something. Waiting for me to do something, like it's that easy. Nothing is ever that easy. And it is all my fault. 'I know what you're thinking but I'm not going to do it.'

Ulana looks at me, then her gaze drops to the cold cigarette end by my black ballet pump. We're sitting on the wall down the alleyway by the chemistry labs. This is where people go to smoke in between class, make out with their boyfriends, or for us, just have a private conversation away from the cafeteria, away from curious ears. Not even the girls' toilets is safe anymore. You never know who will be reapplying their lip gloss or cheek highlighter when you're having a complete mental breakdown about your relationship.

'You have to,' she tells me. Again. 'I know you love him. But he obviously doesn't love you enough to stay faithful to you. Not only did he cheat but he bragged about it. He's embarrassed you at school. Everyone knows.'

My face presses into my palms until I can't feel my nose anymore. 'Ulana, this isn't helping!' I jump down off the wall and press my spine hard against the stone. 'I'm sorry. I don't know why I'm getting angry at you. It's him I'm angry at.'

She jumps down beside me, and wraps an arm around my shoulders. 'It's OK. I get it.'

I tuck my chin and place a hand over my face. I don't want to cry. But I can't stop it. I can't stop Steve from hurting me, I can't stop people from talking about it, and I can't stop the tears from falling down my cheeks.

'Oh Soph!' Ulana turns towards me and pulls me in by my arms. She holds me tight, and I hide my face in the crook of the neck of her red peacock coat. 'Don't cry.'

I've never understood why people say that. It's not like the person sobbing before them will suddenly be able to turn the switch back to Normal mode as soon as those words are spoken. For me, it just makes me want to cry more.

'I…I…' Why won't the words come out?

'I know,' she says.

Does she know? Does she understand? Aiden would never do this to her. But then, I never thought Steve would do it to me. Is she thinking that too? Is she thinking, 'What if it was me?' Or maybe, she's thinking 'Thank God it isn't me.'

When I look up I see Trina Davis standing at the other side of the alleyway, looking right at me. She's by herself. She's always by herself. I wonder sometimes if she gets lonely. That's how I feel right now. Cigarette in hand, she sends a half wave my way. Her eyebrows turned up, she looks like she knows, that she's heard the rumours about Steve too. Everyone probably has at this point. Thank God it's Friday. I just want to get away from this place, from these people. I don't wave back at her. I don't want to be rude, it's not who I am, but I'm worried she'll come over and want to talk, want to hug me too. And then I might crumble in front of her and people will pity me more. Everyone pities me right now, how could they not? I'm pathetic.

'Lunch bell rings in ten. If you're going to do it, you should do it now.'

I look at Ulana who has my bag in her hand. She slips it over my shoulder and nudges me back towards the cafeteria backdoor.

When I go inside, sounds of laughter, ranting, whispering, yelling scattered among smells of grease and fat bombard me at the entrance. No one is looking at me, so I edge further in and skim the crowds for him.

'There he is,' Ulana points out. She stands close behind me.

Steve is sitting with his back to us, beside his friends.

'Should I just wait? I can ask him over to mine later then talk to him properly without everyone here watching the drama unfold.'

'No. Because if he comes over to your house tonight, you're not breaking up with him. You're listening to all his lies, and next week we'll probably be back here with you crying into my shoulder and me telling you that it will happen all over again. Which it will.'

'It could just be a one-off,' I repeat for the fiftieth time since Ulana first told me.

'A "one-off" is one girl, one time. It's not five girls—'

My feet are moving before she's even finished her sentence. They're taking me closer to him. My soles are skimming the floor but I don't feel it. I'm floating and I can't stop.

I'm standing behind him before I can turn back. 'Steve?'

He turns around and feigns a smile across his face. 'Oh, hey.'

'Oh, hey'? That's all I get? After everything?

'Hey,' I mutter back and feel immediately stupid for matching his greeting.

He stares at me waiting for me to speak first. Who is this person sitting here in front of me? This isn't Steve, not my Steve. This is someone else.

'Can we talk?'

'The bell is about to ring. I can't be late again to English.'

'Then I'll talk fast—'

'Not now, Soph. I'll come over later.'

'No, it has to be now. I—'

'I'll text you later.'

'No. I want to—'

The bell rings. Everyone gets up and starts collecting their bags, phones, throwing Coke cans into the blue recycling bin, half-eaten cold lunches into the brown bin, plastic into the green. Why is he getting up? I'm not finished yet. I'm still talking. Why is everything moving so fast? It's spinning like I'm drunk. I grab a chair to steady myself and open my mouth. 'Steve, I want to break up,' I blurt out loudly.

He turns slowly. 'What?'

A couple of his friends start laughing. 'Shut up!' he yells at them. His face reddens, his cheeks turning a warm crimson colour but I keep going.

'It's over between us.'

'Why?' he asks.

Why? He's asking me for a reason?

'You cheated.'

'No I didn't. I told you, stupid rumours. Soph, I—'

'You cheated! I have proof.' I bite my lip and hope he doesn't ask to see it. I don't have anything, but I just want the truth for once.

'Look, it didn't mean anything.'

My chest heaves as I double over. So it is true. I didn't want it to be so badly. I wanted it all to be just a rumour.

'It's not that bad.'

'That's it, it's over.'

I hadn't realised how loud that was. Now a small crowd gathers around us. Steve looks around then turns back to me. He straightens up then casually runs a hand through his hair. 'You know what, Soph? I was done with you anyway. You're nothing but a tease.'

'I'm not a tease!'

He smiles but it's a strange smile. It's a smile that tells me this isn't over. Then he turns his back on me, and walks away, pushing past the crowd that's got bigger.

Ulana grips me by the arm. 'You did it. It's over.'

But it doesn't feel over.

It feels strange. Not right. As if I'm inside someone else's body and they're in control. They're speaking for me, they're ending it with Steve. But I don't want that. I don't want to lose him.

'Come on,' she says, pulling me towards biology.

When we get there, I see Steve's friend Barker in the back row. He's smiling. It's that same smile though. Why is he looking at me like that? What does he know?

The afternoon drags on but Steve's smile lingers in my mind. Then I see his eyes, his hair, that little dimple in his chin just off to the left. I miss him. I miss him so much.

I hurry home when the bells rings at 3.10 p.m. I can't cry again at school. So I rush back, drop my bag at the base of the stairs, and collapse onto my bed. I pull the rose pink blanket up over my head and surrender to the darkness where it's safe and warm.

I can't stop seeing his face, replaying the fight at lunch over and over again. I'm so stupid. I shouldn't have said anything at all to him. If I hadn't, he'd be here with me now. Holding me. Kissing me. Telling me how sorry he is. And I'd be able to forgive him. I would. I already forgive him.

I'm so stupid.

It's all Ulana's fault. She got me so worked up outside. She doesn't know our relationship. We would have got past this. It would have made us stronger, closer.

But what if she's right, what if it happened again? And again?

How many times could I forgive? How many times would he ask me to forgive?

My phone beeps. It's not 'Love' by Lana del Ray so it's not Steve.

Why isn't it Steve?

My temples ache so I coax them gently to relaxation with my fingertips. But I can't relax. There's so much in my mind that won't let me be. It hurts so much. Everything. Well, mostly just everything to do with Steve.

I glance at my phone screen without unlocking it. It's

not Steve. I already knew that so why do I feel so disappointed that Ulana is texting me, and not him?

I don't want him to text me.

He hurt me. He used me. He humiliated me. He cheated on me.

I DON'T WANT HIM TO TEXT ME.

But…I do want him to text me. I want him to come over and tell me how sorry he is and how much it was a mistake. Better yet, I want him to convince me and everyone at school that it's not true. It's a rumour that's not true because he would never cheat on me. He loves me.

Does he love me?

Does he know how much I love him?

My phone rings again, reminding me there is still an unanswered message waiting for me in my inbox that's not from Steve. I give in and press my thumb down hard on the ID touch.

Are you at home?

My thumb moves quickly across the keypad.

Yeah, why?

Check Steve's Facebook page

I don't move. My eyes skim the bedroom until they rest on the pink laptop sleeve on the armchair in the corner. But I don't get it. My phone beeps again. It's still Ulana.

Are you on it yet? I can't believe he would do that to you. Why does he even have photos like that of you anyway?

My upper body moves faster than my legs and I spill out onto the floor. Scrambling up, I yank the laptop towards me. Curled up like a tight ball, I kneel over and type quickly into the search engine.

My phone screen lights up once more. *Sophia?*

Facebook. Steve…I click on his name from an old post on my wall and jump right into his profile. I don't see the profile picture that he's updated to display just his face. I've been cut out from that photo, even though I'm there. I don't see that he's changed his status from 'In a Relationship with' to 'Single'. I don't see that there have been over 220 comments under the photo he posted less than three hours ago.

No. I see only the photo.

Of me.

Me.

I'm naked.

My body is completely exposed except for the lace underwear. It's there for everyone to see, for everyone to comment on.

He's Facebook friends with 2,467 people.

2,467 people.

My phone is beeping beside me somewhere on the rug. Somewhere beside me, or under me. I don't know where anything is anymore. Where anything belongs anymore.

What's happening? Did you see it?

I can't breathe.

Hello?

I can't see. Everything is so blurry.

We need to report him

I'm going to be sick.

This has to be illegal?

Everything is slipping away, the light from the bedroom, the light from the laptop screen, the light from the phone, the light from…from…

LUCY

'Lucy?'

'Hmm?' I look up and see Lily looking at me, carrot stick still caught in between her fingers.

'Did you hear a word I said?' she says, finally taking a bite.

'Oh. Sorry, did you say something?'

'Only for the last ten minutes!' Mollie giggles and splits her sugar packet, half the contents spilling out on the table around her latte. She mutters under her breath then gets up to find more.

'Are you feeling OK?' Cara asks.

'Yeah, why?'

'You just look a little pale. Still hungover from Saturday night?'

'Actually, I'm not feeling a hundred per cent. Maybe I am still hungover,' I say, knowing that I spent all night with only apple juice in my wine glass, just in case – wait, just in case? What does that mean? 'Um, I probably just didn't sleep well last night or maybe I'm coming down with a cold.' A plate of mashed potatoes and buttered beans sits in front of me, steam no longer rising. I'd thought I'd wanted it when I sat down to eat it, but now I suddenly couldn't remember why I was craving it in the first place. Just the sight of it made me want to throw up. And that smell. My mouth waters and I feel nausea surfacing.

'You didn't eat much today,' Cara points out, nodding to my plate.

'Yeah, I'm not surprised. Who orders mash and beans for lunch?' snorts Mollie as she plops down in her chair with a large handful of small brown sugar packets. She must be anticipating several more attempts at opening one.

'I thought it looked good but it's actually gross.' I slide the plate away from me. Something pink and sparkly catches my eye and I think I see Trina Davis at the other end of the room. I instantly feel the blood boiling inside me and squint to look again. But it's not. As I turn back to my tray, she appears from behind a large crowd of fifth-years.

'And I thought you looked rough,' scoffs Cara.

Trina perches on the edge of a long table, her tray empty except for a takeaway cup of coffee. Her face is red and puffy, and her hair is scraped back in a low bun.

She's swallowed up in a baggy navy jumper and leggings that make her legs look like sticks. I barely recognise her from the Trina from Saturday night. The one that danced wildly, and swigged vodka from the bottle, and flirted with Rhys at the party – the one that almost risked everything. As if he can hear my thoughts, he appears from behind the fifth-years too and immediately heads for her table. I want to rush over there and yank her off that bench by her hair before he reaches her. Maybe no one will notice, and I can go on pretending that there's a real chance that Rhys and I will get back together.

Like there's any chance now.

Not now. Not with—

'Is that Trina with Rhys again?' blurts out Mollie, another sugar packet spilling out between her fingers. Why is it so difficult for this girl to open a small paper envelope of sugar?

Cara and Lily both turn in that direction and a couple of nosy girls at the next table look over too. Mollie's voice tends to carry far, even in a busy cafeteria.

'What is he doing?'

'Doesn't he know you're right here? You can see them. We all can. That's so disrespectful.' Cara looks at me, waiting, her eyes wide.

What does she expect me to do?

Lily waves another carrot in the air, gesturing towards their bench.

They clearly all expect me to do something. And if I don't, they'll know something is different about me.

They'll know about It.

Before I can stand, I see Rhys and Trina get up from the table. He's trying to say something to her but she's backing away from him, not waiting until he's finished talking. Maybe they're fighting. That's perfect. Then I don't have to do anything at all, I can just – oh no, she's coming this way. I feel it again. Blood. Boiling. Some kind of weird sensation in my belly – what is that?

'Well?' Lily says, turning around to see how far she is from our table.

She's close. But I wait until she gets a little closer…just a little closer…there. I jut my foot out sharply, cracking into her ankle and through her legs. She grunts and goes down, fast and hard, to the ground. Her shoulder bag slides out in front of her, contents spilling out everywhere. When she peels herself off the ground, I'm impressed to see she's still holding her coffee cup. Even though the entirety of its contents is on the ground. And all over her jumper. It soaks through the fabric and clings to her chest.

Mollie starts squealing, followed by Cara and Lily. Then most of the cafeteria.

I hadn't meant to kick her that hard. I watch as she slides onto her knees and starts frantically shoving everything back in her bag, her cigarettes the last to go in. She inches up to standing, careful not to drop anything in front of me again. Her right knee is slightly bleeding, having hit the tile floor first. A twinge pulls at my stomach, but I push it away.

She deserved this.

I don't know why, but she deserved this.

Her cheeks are red, and she takes a step towards me, but doesn't follow through. Her eyes drop to the ground and she pushes past me. She rushes out the door, bag smacking off the handle as she flees. I hear a noise escape her lips before she disappears round the corner. Is she crying? I don't think I kicked her that hard…did I?

'Bye Trina!' Cara yells after her. I force myself to smile along with her, with my friends, even though I don't feel victorious in any way. Glancing over at Rhys' empty table, I take a deep breath. If he'd been here, if he'd seen, I'd have lost my chance with him forever. Which could still happen if…if… 'I'm skipping the rest of the afternoon,' I announce, swinging my bag over my shoulder. I can't go on like this. I need to know. I need to be sure.

'Ooh, can I skip with you? Shopping? Cinema? I'm dying to see the new Zac Efron movie. I hear he gets shirtless like ten minutes into it. Bonus!' Mollie claps.

'He's kinda old now,' shrugs Lily.

'Sorry not today…I'm meeting my mum in town.' When I slide off the bench, I see Trina's pink lipstick still lying on the ground by the table legs. I don't know why but I pick it up and drop it into my bag.

I walk out the same door Trina ran through and take the same path. But while she probably took a right through the woods to go smoke in the clearing by the chemistry lab, I go left towards the main centre.

I walk past the chemist on the high street and cross over to the bus stop. I can't go in there for what I need. I can't risk seeing someone that recognises me. So I wait for the 67 bus.

A cold breeze stabs through my coat as raindrops start to fall all around me. I haven't brought an umbrella, so I step back under the shelter. But I suddenly don't want that dry comfort. I want to feel the rain. I want to feel it on my hands, my fingertips, on my cheeks. It tangles in my hair and trickles down the strands, finally resting on my shoulders. But it doesn't cool me. It doesn't extinguish the heat searing in my stomach. The only thing that can do that is a Negative sign on that pregnancy test.

When the bus arrives, I drop a couple of pounds into the red plastic tray and weave my way to the back, avoiding curious faces and watchful eyes. It only takes eleven minutes to get to the next town, through a winding maze of country lanes, 'bend ahead' signs and single-lane roads. I don't look out the window. I don't see the fields go by, or the sheep grazing, or the cows sleeping. I don't count the red cars like I used to with my dad when I was little, that I still do now when no one is watching me. No. I stare at my hands the entire eleven minutes. I squeeze patches of skin with my fingers and watch as the skin whitens then goes red. And I try to calm the volcano that's erupting inside my mind.

I try to coax it back to the Glen Affric camping trip. To the ochres of deep oranges and rusted browns that meet overhead. To the sizzling hot grill awash with hot dogs and salted corn on the cobs. To my parents sitting side by side under the crystal clear night sky, exchanging the occasional romantic glance when they think I'm not watching. I try to ease my thoughts back to those simpler times.

But my mind fights back. And when we pull into the main centre, I claw my way to the front and escape back into the rain, feeling it once again trickle over me. Then I cross the street, take a left up Upton Road, and a right through the door of Superdrug. I pass the tiny glass bottles of shimmery nail varnish, tall tubes of strong-hold hairspray, multi-coloured coiled hairbands, pin-like kirby grips, and feathery wands of jet black mascara. I go to the back. The very back.

It's funny how shops always place the pregnancy tests at the back. Is it for privacy? Or is it to shame the young unwed girls who have to walk through the entire store to get to it, with their heads tucked to their chins, cheeks a warm red, repeating a silent prayer that no one will see them, that no one will notice their sins?

I'm doing that walk of shame right now. My head is tucked to my chin and my cheeks are no doubt as red as those crimson nail gels up front. Rectangular boxes loom over me. Loaded onto shelves that reach from the ground near my toes up to the ceiling where a too-bright fluorescent light burns my retinas. Dozens of boxes neatly packed, some with smiling (married) couples, one with a blue bird soaring over the pink label, and another with a small white house in the corner. Each cover represents something I don't have. Something I won't be able to give…It. A parent. No, *two* parents. A house.

What does the bird represent? Freedom? (Bit ironic isn't it?)

There are just so many options. Which do I get?

One shows a smiley face if it's Positive so I quickly push that one aside. Another is triple the cost of the rest, so I choose the one with the biggest display sign. That must mean it's in high demand, which means it's the most accurate. And I need accuracy. I need a hundred per cent accuracy.

My hands tremble when I slide over the ten-pound note, but the cashier doesn't even look at me. Perhaps she knows my dilemma all too well herself. She looks a little like Trina which makes me blush even more. She has the same hair colour as her, wears the same shade of lipstick – too shimmery for daytime. Perhaps this is where Trina will be in a year. While we all go to university, she'll be here, selling girls like me pregnancy tests.

Or maybe it won't be her standing behind that counter. Maybe it will be me. And maybe I'll have a baby inside my belly.

'Your receipt.'

I shake my head and glance up. Now she's looking at me. Right at me. 'Sorry, what did you say?'

'Do you want your receipt?' she says again.

'No.' I snatch the box from her. 'Thank you.' I can't have any evidence on paper that I was here. Nothing that anyone can find. And use against me.

When I get home, it's stopped raining but the dark clouds still hover high above. Clusters of charcoal grey and swirls of white tell me that it will probably shower again tonight. My mum's car is gone from the driveway, which is odd but I don't question it too much right now. I'm glad to get the privacy. I know I'm safe to do this, for now.

The first thing I do is drink two large glasses of water.

But when I'm on the toilet I can't go. I'm too nervous.

So I go back downstairs and drink another glass of water. Then I jump up the stairs. Run around the coffee table. Push my stomach with cold fingers. Soak my hands under a warm tap. But it's staring at the running tap that finally does it.

I dangle the stick in the toilet bowl, feeling the warmth

graze my fingers. But it doesn't gross me out. It's too late for that. I wash my hands and set the timer on my phone, balancing it on the edge of the sink.

Then I wait.

And wait.

What now?

I grab the box for instructions, but my fingers are clammy and it slips out dropping on the floor. Collapsing onto my knees, the words on the back jump around so I have to focus my eyes and read the sentence over and over again.

One vertical line = Good. Not Pregnant.

Two vertical lines = Not Good. Definitely Not Freaking Good. Bad. Very Very Bad.

Please not two lines.

Please not two lines.

I turn the stick over in my hand, my eyes still up towards the clock. Slowly lowering them, I see the shelf above the bath with the small apothecary jars of lavender bath salts and rosehip bath oil. Then the tip of the bathtub. Then the bottom. The black tile, the white tile, the black tile…the…the…

Two vertical lines.

Two.

Not Good.

Definitely Not Freaking Good.

ULANA

I check the hallway again. No Aiden. No Sophia. I knew she wouldn't be in today, but Aiden? He never misses class.

One of the other girls rounds the corner and leans against the wall outside the classroom doors of the chemistry wing. Her brown shoulder bag flops on the ground, her pink phone case sticking out the side pocket, gold feather attached to the top clip. She reminds me of Sophia, but I think her name is Clare, maybe with an 'i'. I don't know, not many people talk to me here, except Sophia. She was one of the first people I met at Birchwood, after Trina Davis. Both of them were so warm and welcoming, especially Sophia. She was so kind to me. I thought everyone here would be like her. I was wrong.

Clare looks up at me then goes back to looking at the dark red hue on her fingertips. My parents would never let me wear a nail varnish that shade, or any shade at all. They hate the look of varnish on girls. They're better about make-up; I get away with some blotting powder, lip balm, and occasionally a little mascara. I've never tried eyeliner or lipstick before. Maybe one day I'll try. Bold lined eyes. Lashings of the blackest blacks of mascara. I've seen women like that back in Morocco. Their made-up eyes pop out from brightly coloured yards of silks and chiffons.

The door suddenly opens and hits me in the elbow. 'Oh sorry, Ulana,' says Mr Fergusson.

'No, it's my fault, Sir. I shouldn't have been standing right at the door.' I bend down and slide my bag across the floor before heaving it up over my shoulder. It's heavy, with every textbook imaginable to a school syllabus. That's what I carry around with me most days just in case I need to cross-reference anything, or I get a few minutes between class to read up on next week's assignment. Or sometimes next month's. I know people must think I'm weird but it's easy for them. For me, one bad grade is the beginning of a very long discussion that ends with my parents re-evaluating their decision to move the family to the UK for its education system and 'Western opportunities'.

I know I'm lucky to be living here, to be educated here so I can't afford to mess that up. After school is university and then I will be a doctor just like my dad was, I mean 'is'. I know he's ashamed that he's not anymore but it's not his fault. He works hard to provide for us. He would do anything for me. I'm the one that should be ashamed. I lie to him every day. The truth is I don't know how he'd react to Aiden. He's such a compassionate man, and he raised me to be kind to others. But I'm terrified he won't approve, that the same concerns that I have he'll have too, and the not knowing if that will happen is just not enough for me to take that risk. So I do everything I can to keep these two lives that I've found myself living as separate from each other as possible.

Home. School.

Family. Aiden.

Neither can meet.

I make lists, sometimes, of the lies I would tell if I was ever caught out:

1. *I've never met him before in my life.*
2. *He's in my class at school, he was just asking me about the essay due.*
3. *He offered to walk me home. Through the woods (that's not weird at all).*
4. *I heard a noise from the woods so went to check it out. With Aiden (again, not weird).*
5. *OK, fine, but this is the first time anything like this has ever happened.*
6. *We've only hung out twice, maybe three times, that's it.*
7. *I've never met him before in my life.*

But like I said, neither can meet so hopefully I'll never have to refer back to that list. Home stays there, school stays here. And that includes Aiden. If only he could understand that. I yank out my journal and stare at the deep black lines on the pages. I'm about halfway in with scribbled notes but today I have something else to write on these pages. Today, I'll write him a letter. I'll explain everything, I'll help him understand. My hands hover above the journal as words jump around in my head. Where do I start? 'I love you'?

I glance around as if people can hear my thoughts, know what I just said to myself. Love. No, it can't be love? I can't love him. And Aiden can't love me. Our relationship means so much to me of course, but love is different. Love means marriage, maybe. Love means... public acknowledgement. We are definitely not tackling that just yet.

Yet? I just said Yet. That must mean that it probably will happen eventually. So why not just do it now while we're still somewhat under the radar. Quick lunch in the daytime, no lingering. It could be done, theoretically. I think. Sophia could come round, 'pick me up' for the full effect. I leave with her, come back a couple of hours later and no one would have to know how exactly I filled those couple of hours and with who...with whom?

While Mr Fergusson demonstrates a rather inde-cipherable chalk model of molecules and cluster cells on the blackboard, I craft a very indecipherable letter to Aiden. At first it weakly consists of lots of 'I'm Sorry' but soon moves on to what he really wants to hear, and what I really want to say.

It is worth the risk.

What we have is worth the risk.

What I don't write is 'What we have is worth *any* risk' because that's a statement I'm not ready to be tested on. Any risk implies complete and full disclosure to my parents. I can't do that. But I now have to consider that there will be a time when Aiden does ask me to do that. And then his question really will have to be answered – are we really worth the risk?

By the time the bell rings for lunch, my letter is neatly folded into three sections and tucked between my textbooks. Sliding them off the table, something knocks me, sending everything to the floor. 'Hey!' I yell, as the figure steps over me.

'Sorry, but you were in the way,' he says, glancing back, hands still tucked into his pockets. 'Your head scarf must have been over your eyes.'

I roll my eyes and quickly gather up my strewn belongings on the floor. I hurry down the hallway under the throbbing of the lunch bell. I know she's not here today but I push open the doors into the cafeteria hoping to see Sophia's smiling face. Instead, all I see is Clara from her drama class.

'Hey, have you seen Sophia?' she asks me, clutching a copy of *As You Like It* in her hand.

'No, she's…um…absent today.'

She turns and a sympathetic smile inches onto her face. 'Yeah, I guess I would be too.'

'Oh, you heard?' I feel nauseous. Why are so many people talking about this today? Sophia must be going out of her mind. I'll stop by after school, tell her no one mentioned it today. I hate lying.

'Yeah, I think everyone at school saw those photos. It's disgusting that he did that. That must be a crime.'

'Yeah, I said that too.'

'Well, if you talk to her, tell her we're all thinking about her. No girl will go near him now. Well, except one I suppose.'

'Wait, who?'

Clara rolls her eyes, 'Lily Shepherd is telling everyone that she and Steve hooked up at the weekend. Twice.'

Great. As if Sophia needs this too. Blood searing hot inside me, I spot Steve sitting at a table in the way back. By the time I push through the lunch crowds, I'm suddenly right there beside his chair. He turns to face me, and I immediately notice Aiden next to him. It's too late to turn back. 'Have you talked to Sophia? Apologised?' I ask Steve. He ignores me but his eyes flicker to the ground. His cheeks redden slightly. I open my mouth to say something else, something that will really get his attention but then I see Aiden. He seems to be looking at a piece of paper flat out on the table. My piece of paper. That's my writing. That's my letter.

I turn back to my textbooks, my eyes searching for the letter I once held but it's no longer there. It must have dropped out when that guy bumped me. Yes, I wanted Aiden to read it but not the entire Sixth Year too.

'What's that?' My voice hitches a little at the end and I hope no one notices.

'Aiden here got a love letter,' laughs Lee. 'Listen to this, *Aiden, I want you to know how much I care about you and how important you are to me. You're sweet and—'*

'I think I've heard enough.' I'm going to throw up.

Aiden tries to snatch the letter from Lee's hands, but he pulls it back too quickly and passes it on to Steve.

'You're so patient and understanding—'

'Haven't you got better things to do, like deleting those photos of Sophia from your profile pages?' I blurt out. Then I turn and walk out the cafeteria, my shoes loudly stomping the tiled flooring underneath my soles.

I'm burning inside. The humiliation courses through my veins. How dare they read that letter like it's some kind of joke? There are real emotions in there. *My* emotions are in there.

Am I a joke to them? Am I a joke to Aiden? And why isn't Sophia responding to my texts?

TRINA

<u>Journal Entry 4: 10.10.2018</u>

~~Saturday~~

~~On Saturday, I~~

~~Something happened to me. Something horrible happened to me. It wasn't my fault. It wasn't my fault.~~

~~Wasn't my fault~~   ~~Was my fault~~   Is my fault

I don't know if I can write this.

I can't.

I won't.

I'm done with journals. They mean nothing. Just words. Trivial feelings I once felt. But I don't feel that way anymore. I don't have those words in my head anymore.

Everything is so different now. Nothing is as it was before.

Before…

What if someone was to find this? What if my mum

was to read this, if she was interested at all in what I was thinking, what I was feeling? What then? There would be questions. The police would want to talk to me. They would ask me to come to the station and make a statement. I've seen TV shows. That's how it works. And even then, people like Him get away with it all the time. They'll blame me. All they have is questions.

Questions.

Those questions would need answers and I don't have those. I don't know what happened on Saturday night. And then they'll blame me. Say it was all my fault. Everything is always my fault. I do everything wrong. I mess up all the time. I can't get anything right.

I don't know what happened.

I don't know anything.

All I know for sure is that my life ended on Saturday. My old life that is. It ended and a new one began. And not one I'd ever wish upon anyone to live.

I'm not making any sense.

It's because nothing makes sense to me anymore. Nothing is right anymore. Everything is wrong. So wrong.

I guess if anyone ever reads this, I should at least try. I'll try to explain. Where should I start?

Maybe I should start at the beginning.

Saturday was like any other day for me. My mum works shifts so she's hardly ever home, and when she is all she does is sleep. I can't fault her for that. She's doing her best. She's single-handedly keeping a roof over our head and a meal on the table for us. I work a little, answering the phone at the taxi rank a few afternoons a week and at the weekends, but I only make just over four quid an hour. That doesn't get us far. But I give most of it to my mum, putting it in the empty tin of Quality Street in the bottom kitchen cupboard where she keeps all of her money. She says banks are for people who have money, not people who need it, and especially not those who use it almost immediately after they earn it.

So on Saturday, as usual I put my earnings into the tin, expect for one ten-pound note which I spend on a cheap bottle of wine from Aldi's and one pack of cigarettes which I try and stretch out over the week at school and on the walk home. I'm usually at a house party on the weekends, so I just bum a smoke off anyone that's there.

That's what I was doing when I met him – Him. He was smoking outside, and I wanted to save my pack for the week, so I lied and said I had just run out. He slid his carton out of his jeans pocket and popped the lid open for me to take one. I pulled out two and tucked the second one behind my ear for later. He thought that was cute. I thought He was cute.

I wouldn't have even been talking to him if Rhys hadn't ignored me. I went there, in my new clothes from H&M – which I can't return now because...

Because.

Anyway, I see Rhys there sitting on the armchair in the living room next to the iPod dock, can of beer in his left hand, while his right hand wraps around the waist of Lucy McNeil. Yep, she was sitting on his lap, with her tongue down his throat.

After that, I spent twenty minutes crying in the toilet while some random hugged me and told me 'Boys are really simple. Just make him jealous – flirt with someone else and he'll be all over you again soon.' So I did just that. I picked someone. The guy outside smoking Camels. He was older, one of Lee's brother's friends who just showed up uninvited, and he seemed worthy of making Rhys jealous.

But I was wrong.

I was so wrong.

We started drinking more. He'd brought vodka and rum, and I began drinking everything he gave me. I was drunk. I knew I was drunk. The room was moving in front of me, pulsing like it was alive or something, and I couldn't stop banging into people when I walked. I fell on the stairs a few times as I climbed up with Him. I've never been that drunk before but I remembered when my mate Ana was she stuck her fingers down her throat and said she felt better after. I tried but I couldn't make myself throw up in the toilet. So I staggered into one of the bedrooms and lay down on the bed. I thought if I slept it off for an hour then I would wake up and feel a bit more sober. Sober enough to walk home anyway. But until then I couldn't go back like that. My mum would kill me. And I did fall asleep for a little bit. I think. But, when I...

When I.

When I woke up, I wasn't alone in the bedroom anymore. The first thing I noticed was the H&M skirt. Navy with embroidered pink roses. It was on the floor beside the bed. It wasn't on my body anymore. My shoes were beside it. My tights. My tights were ripped. I could see the fabric frayed and split. All I thought at that moment was why are my tights ripped?

And then I felt Him. And it was happening. It was happening to me. But I didn't want it to happen. So I started saying No. But he wouldn't stop. He told me to shut up. But I didn't shut up. I started screaming. Because it hurt.

It hurt so bad.

And he wouldn't stop.

And then I couldn't scream anymore because his hand was over my mouth. My face was so wet, and I realised after that I had been crying.

I had been crying and he wouldn't stop.

I said NO and he wouldn't stop.

And there was blood.

My blood.

Because what he hadn't known at the time – or maybe

he didn't care – was that until that party, I was a virgin. And I wanted to stay that way until I fell in love.

That sounds so stupid now.

So childish.

I can see that now.

I was a child before Saturday and I'm not now. Because of Him. He stole that from me. And I hate him.

But mostly, I hate myself.

They'll say it was my fault. My fault. All my fault.

They'll say it was because I was drunk.

They'll say it was because I wore a short skirt.

Because I had make-up on, red lipstick, black eyeliner – adult make-up.

Because my top was low-cut.

Because I wore a lace bra.

Because

Because

Because it's always the girl's fault. Never the guy's. And most certainly, always <u>my</u> fault.

<u>I HATE MYSELF.</u>

SOPHIA

'Steve!' I hurry after him but he quickens his footsteps. He dodges oncoming students, dipping his shoulder back to swerve around them, stepping to the side to pass them. He moves so gracefully, so calculated. As if we're all pieces in a game that's he manipulating. Is that what I was? A game piece to shift around the board then toss to the side when he was done. If so, what was the game? Maybe I know the answer to that already. Perhaps I always knew it.

'Steve!' My feet dance around bags on the floor and shoes in my path – ballet flats with bows on the front, Converse hightops, Keds, leather ankle boots, until finally I catch up to him. 'Stop avoiding me!'

He spins around causing me to stumble into him slightly. His hands catch me by the hips to steady me and I'm suddenly nose to nose with him. The flutter in my stomach reminds me that this is Steve. My Steve.

The Steve with the hugs, with the words, with the kisses, with all the promises. The Steve who snuck out halfway through Star Wars which he had been dying to see for months, just to get me more popcorn after I spilled mine on the floor. The Steve who knows how excited I get when eggnog lattes appear on Starbucks' winter festive menu. The Steve who walks me to French after the lunch bell rings just so we can spend an extra three or four minutes together. The Steve who, knowing how much of a Francophile I am, bought me *The Greatest Hits of Juliette Greco* on CD for my birthday. We even talked about visiting Paris one day. When we were older. When we were married.

But the expression in his eyes tell me this is not that Steve, not My Steve. This is someone else. Someone I wish I'd never met. Someone who's destroying my reputation on social media just to get back at me for breaking up with him in front of everyone. Someone who posted private photos of me that I trusted him with. Someone who's hurting me, making me cry, making me feel ashamed.

And then the flutters disappears. Just like that.

I move his hands away and steady myself against the wall, before turning back to face him. 'You haven't been responding to my texts.'

'I've been busy,' he shrugs.

'Yeah I know. Steve, what are you doing? Take the photos down. Why would you post them?'

'I didn't post them.'

'I saw them on your Facebook profile. Everyone saw them!'

'Yeah, but I wasn't the one who posted them in the first place. Euan and I were messing around and he saw the photos on my phone and posted them from there. You know I never keep passwords on my apps. I'd never remember them.' He shifts his bag to the other shoulder, and rocks back on his heels. 'I have to get to class. I can't be late again.'

I gently touch his arm to stop him leaving, and lean in. 'So you're saying you didn't post them yourself. Your friends did?'

'Yep.'

'So take them down.'

'I did.'

'No, you didn't. They're still up!'

'Are they?'

He smiles slightly and I wonder why I ever felt a flutter at all for him.

'Take them down,' I say again.

'I'm really busy after school today.'

'I'll report you on Facebook, then your account will get deleted permanently. That's what happens. I Googled it.'

'You Googled it?' he laughs.

He's laughing at me.

He's not even taking this seriously. He thinks it's

funny. He thinks I'm funny. Tears pool in my eyes and I feel them spill over, running down my cheeks. Then I see it, just a glimmer in his eye, almost like he feels bad for me, that he feels guilty for what he's done. But before I can speak again, before I can appeal to that side of him, to that Steve, to My Steve. His friends appear from around the corner.

'Hey Sophia! Here to do a little dance for us?' laughs Euan.

'Wait, wait…let me get my phone out so I can take more photos,' says Lee.

Then Steve joins in, and once again, he's gone. Everything I once knew about him, once loved about him, is gone. They're still laughing as I run down the hallway away from them, tears spilling out.

When I clear the edge of the hallway and round the corner, an impact hits me like a wall and I stumble to the ground. Climbing onto my hands, I immediately recognise the brown suede ankle boots in front of me. I finally gaze up.

'You almost knocked me over.'

Lucy's bag lays strewn beside me. Notebooks, pens, a heart-shaped mirror with lilac and rose stars all over the back.

'What are you doing?'

'I…I…Steve.'

Lucy's eyes shoot up and she scans the hallway. 'Where?

I don't see anyone?' Her eyes dart back down to me, still on the ground. 'Don't just sit there. Help me pick up my stuff. It's your fault it's all over the floor.'

I start sweeping her things into the middle, in front of me.

She drops her hands down to her hips. 'Don't just scoop it into a pile. You're gathering up all that hallway dirt. Pick up each thing, brush it off using your top and put it back inside my bag.'

Knees aching, I stay down. Her Revlon Peach Parfait lipstick trembles in my fingers, and drops to the ground again.

'Careful! That shade is almost impossible to find. If it breaks, I can't use it.'

Hot tears prick at my eyes again and I turn my face away so she doesn't see.

'Why don't you help her? Instead of just standing there.' The voice is familiar to my ears – sharp, accent on the rough side, lazy on the T's. When I finally glance up, lipstick still in hand, I see Trina Davis standing over me.

Lucy's face turns white and her eyes flicker. 'Why don't you keep walking and stop sticking your nose in everywhere.'

Trina opens her mouth to respond, then her eyes skim to the floor and she softly shakes her head. She pulls me up to my feet. 'Leave it, Sophia. Let her pick it up herself—'

'What's going on here, girls?' Eyes locked on Lucy and Trina, Miss Fiona, the teaching assistant in Mr Brown's class, walks towards us.

'Nothing. I was just walking to class,' smiles Lucy, flashing teeth whiter than porcelain.

'Then you'd better hurry up and get there. Second bell rang a few minutes ago.'

Lucy hesitates before bending down to scoop her things into her bag. She clenches her jaw, her face hardening to a rock, then hoists the bag over her shoulder. She glances back at Trina then to me, before pushing through us. She mutters something under her breath but I can't hear her. It seems Trina does because she rolls her eyes and shakes her head.

She starts walking with me down the hall. At first she doesn't say anything, she just mirrors my slow and cautious footsteps. Then she eventually looks up at me. 'So what did you do to get on her bad side?'

I tuck my fingers under the shoulder strap of my bag and keep them there. The fabric sits heavy on my skin, the bag weighed down with textbooks and a French paper that I was too ashamed to hand in. I'm better at French than this. But I haven't been able to concentrate this week. Every time I sit down to study, my phone beeps. And every time it beeps, the words on my screen weigh heavy in my mind, like the bag I carry. Ulana made a list for me to follow, when I didn't know what to do. I still don't know what to do. But her list tells me:

A. Turn off my notifications
B. Silence the ringtone
C. Turn off the vibration alerts
D. Deactivate my social media accounts
E. Do whatever it takes to not fall apart, and especially not in public, and not in front of Steve

OK, the last item I put on there myself. But again, nothing works. Because again, I don't know what to do. And when I think I know, it never seems to be the right thing. Like today, when I thought I could reason with Steve. When I thought he'd take one look at me and immediately break down and tell me he was sorry and that he would take down all the posts. And then maybe we'd get back together and erase from my memory the worst month of my life. But no, that didn't happen. He behaved exactly the opposite of what I thought would be the outcome of that conversation. Or, perhaps, he behaved exactly how I thought he would.

I feel Trina's eyes burning into me. 'It's OK. You don't have to talk about it.'

I know Ulana was friends with her when they were younger, and I trust Ulana, but I don't know Trina Davis for myself. I don't know if I can trust her. I don't know if I can confide in her. Besides, Lucy hates her. And if I stand any chance of changing this situation, I need to avoid looking like I've teamed up with her enemy in any way. Trina's reputation is done here at Birchwood High School. But I still have a small window to change my fate. This can't be it. I won't get through the year if it is. I won't get through the week.

Trina places a hand gently on my arm and turns me towards her. 'Look, we don't know each other. We never really…socialised I guess, this year. Or the last few years actually. But I know Ulana, and I know you's are close, so if there's anything you need, you know, like if you just want to talk, or rant or whatever, then just let me know. Because I know how you feel. And I know when school gets like this, and it does for everyone at some point, then it can be really isolating.'

Her face is soft. Her eyes glisten slightly, as if she could cry too. Her touch on my arm doesn't feel strange or unfamiliar. It feels comforting, like maybe I could trust her after all.

Her hand drops from me and hits against her side. Then she turns and walks away in the opposite direction. Her walk is slow, controlled. Like me. She looks nervous about what awaits around the corner of the hallway. Like me. She glances back to see if anyone is following her. Also like me.

But there's also nothing about her that's like me.

Because no one can understand how I feel, how alone I really am.

LUCY

I miss you.

My fingers had trembled above the keys before I'd hit Send late last night. My belly had been doing flips. My cheeks burning. My hands sweaty. But I had sent it. Even though I knew it was a risk. Because if he didn't respond, I'd obsess over it more. And guess what?

He hasn't responded. And I'm obsessing.

It's been ten and a half hours and *he hasn't responded.* I know he would have checked his phone in ten and a half hours so that means he's seen it, and he's made the decision not to respond. Why? We had so much fun at the party. It was like old times. Before everything went so wrong. Before Trina came along and ruined everything. Rhys and I would still be together if she hadn't stolen him from me. Had it not been for her, I wouldn't have got together with anyone else and I certainly wouldn't be in this *situation*. This is all her fault. She made It happen. And now It is ruining my life.

I'm sitting in the back row of the classroom waiting for attendance to finish so I can go throw up in the bathroom again. It's already happened twice this morning. Twice I was reminded of this…It inside me. It's not a baby, not yet anyway. So I don't have to refer to it as him or her. Right now, it can stay as It.

Maybe it doesn't have to be anything. And it won't be if I can help it. I can't do this alone. I need someone. I need Rhys.

He would know what to do. He wouldn't leave me alone to sort this out. He would think it's his baby (I'd have to be creative with the date of conception of course) and then everything would be better. He comes from a good family. He's going to be an engineer. He'd support me regardless of what I decide, no, what *we* decide. Because we'd be a 'We'. And I need that more than anything right now. I can't be an 'I' – I need to be part of a 'We'.

Now.

Like I said, it would be a close call with the dates but I could fix that…I think. A few weeks won't make much of a difference unless Rhys does the maths. Which he might. But by then it'll be too late. We'll be together and he won't leave me, not like this.

If only he would respond to my texts. Then we could hurry along this 'We' process.

'Lucy McNeil?'

I glance up to see faces turned towards me.

'Sorry?'

'Say "Here",' whispers Lily, from across the table.

'Oh, yeah. Here…obviously,' I mutter.

'And Lucy?' prompts Mr Brown from the top of the study room.

'Yes?'

'No phones in the classrooms. You know the rules.'

I glance down at the gold iPhone in my hand, the weight suddenly heavy in my palm. Swiping the screen, it flickers to the clock.

Still no response from Rhys.

Sliding the phone back into the side pocket of my black leather rucksack, I turn to Lily and lean in. 'Did you see Facebook last night?'

Lily throws her hand up to her mouth. 'Did Steve post another photo of Sophia?'

'I can't believe you hooked up with him. Gross.'

'I wasn't the only one.'

'That's actually worse,' I laugh, rolling my eyes.

'Ugh.' She playfully hides her face with her hand. 'Did you hear about Trina?'

'Girls in the back, please turn off your voices for the next three minutes,' hollers Brown as he finishes setting up our day on an antiquated blackboard with a stubby piece of green chalk.

'We have assembly this afternoon?' Lily groans.

I sit up in my chair and lean further in. 'What about Trina?'

'You didn't hear this story?'

'I've been a little…preoccupied this weekend,' I mutter. 'But tell me.'

'Of course you were preoccupied. You were probably sucking face with Rhys all weekend.'

'Yeah,' I mumble, refraining from biting my lip.

'Well, you'll love this story.'

I lean across and touch her arm. 'Tell me!'

'Girls!' Mr Brown puts the green chalk down and rests his hands on his hips.

Lily sits back in her chair and goes back to inspecting a poorly completed manicure, likely done at that cheap nail spa she goes to with Mollie on Saturdays. Mum and I get our gels done at the Sheraton Spa in the city centre. Or we used to. Before…before Dad left and we suddenly had to watch our spending. Anyway, we'd never go to that nail place in town. The air bubbles on Lily's fingertips are a dead giveaway.

My toes twitch and curl in my brown suede ankle boots as I wait for the bell. Lily stifles a yawn and shoots me a look when I start to loudly drum my fingers on the table. When the classroom finally vibrates under the ringing of the bell, chairs screech back. We start filing out, but I lock my arm through Lily's and lead her quickly to the front. 'Now, tell me everything!'

'Well, let's just say Trashy Trina lived up to her nickname! I don't think Rhys will be looking in her direction anymore,' she giggled. 'Lee's brother texted me last night that—'

A pang hits my stomach, and I quickly put my fingers up to my mouth.

'Are you OK?'

My hand drops down quickly to my side. 'Just suddenly feeling a bit queasy.'

'Well, you will be after this story. Adam – Lee's brother – said Trina was "putting it about" at the party apparently, to anyone who was interested.'

'Yuck!'

'I know. She slept with at least two of his mates at the party.'

'This is amazing!' I laugh. Perfect. Exactly what I need to end this between Rhys and Trina, whatever 'this' is.

'Oh my God, here she comes!'

I glance up and see Trina walking down the hallway. Pale face, dark shadows under her eyes, hair lank and sitting limply on her shoulders.

She looks at me, waiting. I turn away, pretending to ignore her, then as she's just about to pass, I step in front of her. She stumbles into me then quickly steps back. 'Trina, you look like hell. Even for your standards. Another busy weekend was it?'

Lily giggles beside me.

'Get out of my way,' she mutters, and tries to shove past me, but I side step and block her exit.

'What's wrong? You don't have to hide it. We all know what happened at Lee's party.'

Her face whitens and her eyes water slightly. 'What?'

'You heard me.' I shift and get close to her face. Really close. 'Do you know what you are?'

'Get out of my way!' she screams again, this time loud enough for a couple of girls to stop to see what will happen next.

Then I see Rhys. He's standing behind the girls, close enough to see us but not enough to hear us. I know exactly what he'll do. I wouldn't have to do this if she'd just back off and let Rhys decide for himself. But she's suffocating him, texting him all the time. She was all over him at Lee's party. Her short little shirt, her low top, her dancing. She did this. Not me. This is her fault.

Rhys starts to push past people, to get to me, or maybe to her. I don't know anymore. But I do know that I need him more. I can't go through this alone. So I lean in and whisper one word in her ear. 'Slut.'

She grabs me by the shoulders and drags me down, hurling me against the wall. My back slams against the beige paint, and my feet give out from under me. I let out a dramatic gasp and start rubbing my head, even though she barely touched me. Her weak little arms couldn't actually hurt me. 'Ow! My head!'

Lily bends down and tries to hoist me up, but I swat her away and stretch out a hand to Rhys who immediately leans in to take it. He pulls me up to my feet and turns to Trina.

'What are you doing?' he asks her.

Her face reddens and tears fill her eyes. She grabs her bag from the floor and pushes us out the way, rushing down the hall.

I resist the smile edging across my face and turn to Rhys. 'What a psycho. She just attacked me for no reason! She's probably just embarrassed about what happened at the party. Did you hear?'

Rhys moves to the side and mutters something.

'What did you say?' I call after him.

I grab my bag from the floor and hurry after him. 'Meet you in class,' I say to Lily. When I catch up with him, I grab his arm and gently tug him around. 'Why didn't you text me back?'

He turns to face me but his eyes drop to the floor. 'Sorry, I've just been busy.'

'Liar.' I flick my hair back and wrap my arms around his waist. 'Whatever. Anyway, do you want to come over after school today?'

He shifts under my grasp and inches away from me. 'I can't today.'

'OK, tomorrow?'

He wriggles loose and is now standing further apart from me, his hands down by his sides. He slides them awkwardly into his jeans pockets. 'I don't think so, Luce.'

'But I thought after the party that we'd—'

'Look, I should check on Trina. This isn't like her.' He steps backwards and tries a smile out but then thinks otherwise. It fades, almost as quickly as our brief reconciliation. Then he's hurrying down the hall. Away from me. To her.

Her.

I slide my phone out from my rucksack and lean against the wall. I open up my profiles on Facebook, Twitter, Instagram, Snapchat, everything I have, and start typing. And once I start, I don't stop.

ULANA

'Wow. There are words in here I'd never even say out loud, let alone post on a public forum!' Aiden stares at his phone screen, mouth agape. 'I can't believe how vicious Lucy McNeil is being towards Trina Davis. Look at that post from an hour ago!'

He shows me the phone but I turn my head away.

'Are you still mad? I swear, Ulana, I tried to get that letter from the boys.' Aiden sits beside me on the bench, his body turned into me. 'I didn't want that read out obviously.'

I shift further away, looking out at buildings I don't even notice. 'It was so humiliating.'

'I know. I'm sorry. For me too.'

I turn back to him. 'You were humiliated? I think it was me pouring my emotions out in that letter that got passed around your friends like a…game or something.'

'Everything you said in there, I feel the same so it was

embarrassing for me too.' His knees playfully nudge mine. 'Look, I'm sorry that happened. But I mean what I said, I feel the same. Can we not spend our afternoon talking about my friends? We barely get enough time together as is.'

My body softens into the seat. 'Fine, I'm sorry too. I shouldn't have chanced writing a note in case it got misplaced. I'm just glad I didn't put my name on it.'

Aiden smiles. 'No, but you did put quite a lot of kisses at the end.'

I gently pinch him and watch him laugh and wriggle away. 'One last thing then I'll stop talking about your friends. You have to get Steve to take those photos down. Do you have any idea what will happen to either of them if their parents or the school sees them? They could be expelled. Well, Steve more than Sophia. She didn't do anything wrong except trust the wrong guy.'

'I know. Believe me, I've talked to him about this. He's not taking it seriously.'

'He has to! He posted naked photos of someone online for everyone to see!'

'You should hear the things some of the girls at school have been saying to his face. He deserves all of it. Someone will report him soon on Facebook and they'll be taken down.'

'He shouldn't have to wait for that. He should take them down now because he's hurting Sophia, someone

I thought he once cared about, once loved. Doesn't it bother him seeing her upset like this? Or was he never serious about her to begin with? He was probably only after one thing.'

'You know Steve and I have never really got on. We're friends with the same people, that's it.'

'The whole situation makes me so angry!'

Aiden wraps his arm around my shoulders and leans into me. 'Nervous for Sunday?'

My shoulders stiffen and my mouth feels suddenly dry. Why *am* I so nervous for Sunday?

'Are you worried someone will see you?'

'No,' I shrug. 'I think the plan Sophia and I have is pretty rock solid – if she's still willing to do it with everything going on. I've already told my dad that I'm going to hers for lunch on Sunday and she said she's staying in all afternoon so if they call to check up on me, she'll make sure to answer the phone before anyone else can. And I don't think they'll call anyway. They have no reason to doubt me.'

Those last words linger in my mouth. They have no reason to doubt me because I've never lied to them before. Because I'm a good girl. I'm not this girl.

'You OK?'

'Yeah. What time is it?'

'It's almost quarter past,' he sighs.

'Well, I'll be seeing you on Sunday so we'll get an extra

day together this week.' I lean in and wrap my arms around him, pulling away when I hear rustling among the trees.

'Relax. It's just the wind. No one's there.'

'See you tomorrow at school,' I smile, picking up my bag and heading back down the path to the school. I always leave through the main doors in the front so no one can question where I've been. And Aiden always leaves through the woods. We never walk together. Not even to class. But Sunday, it will be different. I'll be at his house meeting his parents for the first time. Like a normal couple. Normal. Like those girls I see at school. And I have a couple of days to get used that idea, to that fantasy.

The smile is stuck on my face, pressing into my cheekbones, when I see a familiar figure slumped against the doors of the drama department. His hands frantically move across his phone and tiny thin lines are carved into his forehead. The smile quickly drops, as I pick up my pace.

'Steve!' My voice is louder than I'd expected, the sound reverberating off the walls of the hallway.

He looks up and quickly tucks his phone into his jeans pocket.

'What's wrong? Don't want me to see your newest Facebook post? I will soon enough. Aren't you getting tired of this? I know I am.'

He rolls his eyes and kicks at the ground with the toe of his dark grey trainers. 'Don't you have to hurry home, Ulana? Bit late for you to be out. Daddy might get worried.'

'At least I have someone who cares about me.'

His eyes shoot up and I know I've gone too far. I forgot that Sophia told me last year that Steve's dad left when he was younger and that he still struggles with seeing him. A small fluttering in my belly brings heat to my cheeks. I'm disappointed in myself for bringing that up. My mouth parts as I begin to apologise, 'Steve, I—'

'You don't know anything. Stay out of it.' He gestures me away with his hand, like I don't mean anything, like I'm nothing.

The heat returns to my cheeks but this time it's a different emotion I'm feeling course through my body, through my veins. 'Do you have any idea what you're doing to Sophia? This stops or I'll report you!'

He shrugs, yanks his phone from his pocket, and starts walking away from me. 'So, report me.'

'I will!' I yell down the hallway at him. I spin round and march past the nurse's office, until I hit a short boxy lobby. A stained navy rug sits on the ground beneath my soles, a large cluster of pink chewing gum still attached to the corner by the glass cabinet. Framed team photos and gold trophies line the shelf of 'Birchwood's 2017–2018 Achievements.' The 2018–2019 shelf sits empty, awaiting a better year for field hockey, football and rugby. I never understood sports. Why spend the time running after a ball when there's so much knowledge to gain inside a classroom or inside a book? Sports can be played and taught anywhere in the world, but education, the kind that elevates you to a doctor or an engineer, is a privilege reserved for very few countries. That's why we moved here to the UK. For opportunities. For a life. My trophy will never sit on that shelf and I'm just fine with that.

Turning my back to the gold goblets, medals on strings and round pins, I face the welcome window into the headmaster's office. I step closer, my fingers trembling over the door handle. All I have to do is knock and when I tell Mr Tomlinson what's happening it will stop. Immediately. He'll call Steve's parents, and – and – Sophia's parents. Oh. Of course. I can't say anything. Because if I do, Sophia's parents will get called in too. I'd have involved them and Sophia will get in trouble. They'll see those photos. They'll know. And Sophia will never forgive me.

My fingers drop from the handle and I step back slowly until my spine touches the glass cabinet. The trophies loom over my head and a grinning Steve stands beside Aiden in the framed football team photo behind me. I know, because I've looked at that photo a hundred times. Aiden looks really cute in his team uniform.

I shuffle away from the cabinet and out the main doors. Sophia's face sits in my mind all the way home. I don't know what to do to help her. Just being there for her, just being a shoulder to cry on, it's not helping.

It's not enough.

TRINA

I can't breathe.

I can't eat.

I can't sleep.

I can't do all the things I used to. Things that I once liked, that I once found enjoyment from.

When I go into town, I'm back at the party. The crowds. The voices. The laughter. The noise. All that noise. Yet all that silence. As if the world has stopped. As if it's waiting for me. But to do what I don't know. Maybe I'll never know.

When I watch my favourite TV shows, everything reminds me of that night. The short skirt on the actress. The beer in the hand of the guy playing the dad, that actor my mum fancies. The long hair of the girl on *Hollyoaks*. The crying on *I'm a Celebrity Get Me Out of Here*. The cheering and clapping on *Strictly Come Dancing*. Are they clapping at me? Or at him, cheering him on? Egging him on.

When I sit down to eat dinner with my mum, the smells even bring me back to that night. The wine in my mum's glass, the apples in her fruit crumble smell like warm cider, the meat reminds me of the pepperoni pizzas that Lee's brother ordered at midnight. And my mum just asks me, 'What's wrong?' over and over again.

Over.

And.

Over.

What am I supposed to say? How am I supposed to answer that question? Because it's not a simple answer.

Inside, I'm on fire, burning to a charred crumbling crisp until nothing that resembles me remains. But outside I'm below zero, frozen in the same position, never able to break free, to move forward. I'm stuck. I'm trapped.

That's what's happening to me. It's all happening to me again. I relive that night every day, every minute.

When I go to the shops, the sequins remind me of the top that I wore that night to the party, the necklace in Topshop looks like the one I wore. The window display and red letters at H&M remind me there's an outfit from there that I can't take back like I had planned. I can't return it because it's ripped, torn, stained. Like me. It lies hidden in a bag under my bed, at the back, away from hands, eyes, opinions. Not like me. I'm not that lucky. I have to face people. I have to take it.

And when I get home, when I think I'm safe, my phone beeps: 'Have you seen what Lucy posted?'

What gives people the right to post whatever they want on a public forum? They sit behind their screens, safe from the world, and rant horrible things about people that most of them would never have the guts to say to that person's face. Cowards. All of them. Except Lucy. At least what she writes she would say – or has said – to my face at one point. But all those other people who comment on her posts? No, come the next day they say 'Hi' to me in the hallway. They bite their tongues and wait until I pass them before taking out their phones and telling the world what they really think of me.

Cowards.

I can't believe people form opinions so quickly. Actually, of course I do, it's me. They hate me. They call me whatever they want behind my back, and now to my face. Lucy McNeil and that Lily Shepherd. Like she can talk, she stole Sophia's boyfriend from her. Like she should be throwing mud at me. She's tainted by rumours just as much as me, but that doesn't matter. Because Lucy protects her. No one is there to protect me.

I'm all alone. Or at least, that's how I feel every day now.

I actually thought that I would be embarrassed for people to find out. But now I'm angry. Because that's not what happened. They don't understand. They never will. They think what they want about me. Nothing will change that, especially not my words. They mean nothing.

That guy might be guilty for what he did to me, what he took from me. But all those people who pass judgement, who post comments online along with Lucy, who whisper things about me under their breath at school when I walk by, who pass notes about me in class, all of them are just as guilty. Because they're hurting me too. They're taking advantage of me too. They're taking away something from me too. Something that I'll never get back.

I hate school right now.

I asked Mum if I could change schools but she said I can't. That unless I just drop out, I'm stuck there. Why should I have to drop out? Why should they chase me away?

This is all Lucy's fault.

She thinks I stole Rhys, but they were over long before I met him. He never even looked my way before that. He probably didn't know my name, or that we went to the same school. But when he did look my way, it was amazing. He made me feel amazing. Now he avoids me like the rest. He didn't even stick up for me last week when Lucy got in my face. I barely touched her and she flopped to the ground, making pathetic noises. And he didn't ask me if I was OK – why is no one asking me if I'm OK?? Does no one care? I want to stand in the middle of the cafeteria and scream, 'I AM NOT OK!!!'

I will never be again.

I'm so angry. Why am I so angry at everyone all the time?

It's just so unfair.

People like Lucy McNeil will get what's coming to them. I'll make sure of that.

SOPHIA

I throw open the bathroom door and find Trina at the sink, her face red and damp. A paper towel gripped in her hand, she turns back to the mirror and starts scrubbing at her skin. 'Are you OK?' she asks, her voice a higher pitch than usual.

Dropping my bag to the floor, I march into the first cubicle and lock the door. Sliding down, the cold crude plastic against my back, I pull my knees into my chest. The tiled floor is cold and a little sticky underneath my grey skirt. I don't even mind. I can't stay here anymore. I can't keep coming back here day after day, when nothing changes. He's still here. He's still destroying my life. And he doesn't even care. How could I have ever thought that I loved him? I hate him.

The tile creaks and Trina's black buckle boots appear at the bottom of the cubicle door. All I see is boot and an inch of ankle. Black trainer socks peak out from the tip of the boots. A sliver of colour also sticks out on her left ankle, possibly the remnants of an old tattoo. She knocks gently on the door, the vibration enough to slightly rock the loose cubicle latch. 'Sophia?'

Outside I hear the second bell. If my history teacher reads out attendance and I get marked down again for an unexcused absence, he might call my parents. I've been missing a lot of classes lately. I go to school. Every morning. But sometimes I don't go inside. I wait until my mum disappears around the corner in her red Range Rover, then I walk away from the doors, as far away as possible. Until I don't hear the bell, the students, the teachers. Until I don't hear Steve.

Sometimes I do go inside and I stay for a class or two, maybe even half the day. But when lunchtime hits, when all we have to do is sit, eat and gossip, I usually leave. I'm terrified I'll see Steve or hear people talking about me, about my body, calling me that word behind my back. I know they're thinking it even if they don't say it. That one word.

S.

L.

U.

T.

Those photos have cost me. That one split second. That one decision. And now that one word stays with me. Walks the hallways with me, sits beside me in class, stops me from walking into the cafeteria, and is now apparently causing me to fail history and maybe even French too. My favourite subject. And ironically, biology. I guess my extensive understanding of the human body couldn't even save me from a D on my last essay.

'Sophia?'

Leave me alone. I just want everyone to leave me alone.

'Are you OK?'

No. I'm not. I'll never be OK.

She knocks again. And again. And again. Until I eventually slide my hand up to the latch and pull it to the left. The door pops open and now Trina is standing in the doorway. Her black trousers are frayed at the bottom by her boots and hang loosely on her hips. I don't remember the last time I saw her in anything other than a skirt a little shorter than what we're allowed at school. She usually wears more make-up than the entire teaching faculty put together, but today her face is scrubbed clean and her eyes are grey and wide. She has a large purple bruise on her right elbow. She just stands there, looking at me still sitting on the floor of a dirty bathroom. Then she shuffles further in and squats down, her back against the cubicle wall opposite to me.

'Are you OK?' she asks again.

I shrug because I don't know what else to do.

'Did you eat lunch?'

I shake my head and skim the floor with my eyes.

She shuffles around her handbag for a few seconds then pulls out an array of snacks not for the health conscious: bubblemint gum, half a pack of fizzy strawberry laces, and a Double Decker bar.

I shake my head again and turn away before my stomach speaks for me.

'Are you sure? You look like you could do with some food.'

'That's not food.'

Trina smiles. 'She speaks. Thank God. I thought I was going to have to get the nurse.'

'That stuff will rot your teeth,' I add. 'Plus it's all sugar. It's just going to get converted into fat cells eventually.'

Trina rolls her eyes. 'You know way too much about this.'

'I read a lot of magazines.'

'Junk. All of it.'

'No, it's not.'

'Sure it is. Diet this way. No, wait, diet that way. Lose weight by doing these three things. Lose weight by not doing these three things. Eat this. Eat that. Don't even think about eating that. It's all junk.'

My eyes drop down to the floor. The tips of my boots are dotted with flecks of mud. I raise my head and turn an ear to the doorway. The hallway outside is silent. Classrooms will all be full by now. Bags under desks. Chairs pushed back. The SMARTBoard on pause, waiting to awake from Sleep mode to show another dramatisation of the Battle of Bannockburn. Attendance would have been taken by now. The history teacher will be writing a cross beside my name, before handing it to a chosen trusted student to transport it down the hallway to the front office. In a few minutes the office will be cross-checking today's absence with the dozens before this. I bite my lip and hug my knees in tighter.

'Shouldn't you be somewhere right now?'

I shoot her a look. 'Shouldn't you?'

'Yeah, but no one misses me in class. I'm not exactly university bound. No one expects me to actually turn up to class and do the work.'

'Why not?'

She shrugs and pulls out a fizzy lace. Within seconds her lips and chin are dotted with sugar sprinkles as she chews loudly, and with an open mouth. Two of my pet peeves.

'Sure you don't want one? They're really sour. That's how I like them.'

Before I can say no, my hands slowly move up to the open pack. She shimmies one out from the pack and tips it into my outstretched hungry fingers.

'Don't worry. People will get bored soon,' she says, as I chew my fizzy lace wildly. 'You can report him on Facebook, you know?'

'I know.' I do know, but people kept telling me over

and over again as if that's an option I didn't know about. I know I can report him, that I can tell my parents and his, that I can go to the headmaster or my guidance counsellor. I can do all of that. But what I can't do is erase the photos from people's minds or erase the last few weeks from mine.

'Do your parents know?'

I shake my head. They wouldn't understand.

'I know I've said this before but you can talk to me, you know.' The words hang heavy in the air, waiting for me to hungrily reach for them.

But how can I voice my emotions, my fears, when I can't even understand them myself? So instead, I shake my head again, spit out the sweet that's now left a bitter taste on my tongue and fade back into the crowd that roams the hallways, and my nightmares.

LUCY

The waiting room is cold.

I shiver and wrap my grey blazer around me tightly, trapping any warm air. My eyes fall to the pile of magazines on the table in the centre of the room. Metal chairs with blue cushions line the walls and all face forwards, towards the magazine table. Lifting up out of the chair, I lean into the table and start picking through them with a cautious finger. The only ones I notice are:

Parenting Joy.
Mother & Child Yoga.
Cooking For Fussy Children.
What to Expect When You're Expecting.
Building the Ideal Nursery.
Eating Right for You and Baby.

I flick the finger away and plop back into my chair, spine against wall, hands empty. I don't know what I was expecting to find on the table at the Family Planning Clinic. Probably not images of happy childless women in sequin dresses and glossy lipstick on the front covers of *Glamour*, *Vogue* or *InStyle*, advertising the single unburdened lifestyle.

A redhead walks into the waiting room and momentarily gets excited over *Building the Ideal Nursery*. She whips it off the table and plops down in the chair, hungrily consuming every word and every inch of the white wooden cot, pastel-coloured wall, and frilled bunting on the front cover. She glances up and I catch her eye. I immediately become aware that I'm still wearing my school uniform. She doesn't need to say anything to me. It's all there. All in her eyes. Exactly what she's thinking when she looks at me. Exactly what she wishes she could say to me out loud.

I'm such a cliché, I could punch myself. Young, unwed, pregnant schoolgirl. Sitting here in my school blazer, the Head Girl patch sewn onto the breast pocket. I'm supposed to represent leadership, initiative and brains. Right now, I have none. I don't even have dignity. When I can't stand her stares of judgement any longer, I stand up and move to the corner of the room.

Leaning against the white wall, I instinctively smooth down my white shirt and tuck it into the edges of my black skinny jeans, which press roughly against my stomach. I never used to consider my shape or size. I've always been thin. I've always danced. Ballet, jazz, tap, modern. I did it all. But I can't do any of that now. A baggy white shirt under my blazer hides any weight gain better than a tight black leotard. Plus all that moving around might spur another vomit session. But this time much more public. And harder to clean up, I'm sure.

'Stephanie.'

No one glances up. I rock back and forth on my heels, still tugging at my white shirt. I can't seem to get the middle centred.

'Stephanie?'

I glance up and see the receptionist looking at me, pen in hand. 'Oh yeah. Stephanie. That's me.' Swinging my satchel over my shoulder, I follow the nurse into the first room on the left. The rooms are a stark white like the waiting room. Even the chairs match. Thankfully no baby-filled magazines here. No, probably more important things to discuss.

'Hi Stephanie. My name is Joanne and I'm one of the nurses here.'

Faint pearly pink lipstick stains her front teeth but I don't say anything.

'If you don't mind, a urine sample,' she says, handing me a small plastic cup with a pink lid.

'Oh.' I take the cup from her hands, almost dropping

it on the floor. Wiping the clamminess on the sides of my jeans, I follow her to a toilet outside the room at the other end of the waiting room. I have to pass the redhead again. She glances up and watches each step I take until the toilet door but pretends to be looking at the clock on the wall above my head when I look at her.

I feel eyes on me, from her, from the receptionist, from the other girl who just walked in the door. They're all watching me. They're all judging me.

When I squeeze into the tiny cubicle, I slide out of my jacket and hang it up. But when I sit, I can't pee. I'm too nervous. So I shimmy out of the toilet, back into the waiting room.

I approach the receptionist who's reading a magazine on her lap. 'Um, excuse me?'

She tips her head, and shoos away the magazine, letting it drop to the floor. 'There's a water fountain over there.'

Nodding, I hurry over to the fountain and lap up the water that flows freely from the curved spout. I drink as much as I can, resisting the urge to throw it back up. Then return to the toilet, where I've left my bag and coat.

After I pee, I return to the room where the nurse sits and waits for me. 'OK, great. While we wait for it to be checked, we'll fill out a brief questionnaire. Then we can go over your results and talk about your plans. Does this sound OK?'

Before I can in agreement, she pulls out a white form attached to a clipboard and starts filling in my name. I clear my throat and swallow hard.

'How old are you, Stephanie?'

'Seventeen.'

'Your address?'

'Um…'

She glances up.

'Do you need to know that information?'

'You have the option to put "Anonymous" or "Not Applicable" for any question.'

'OK, um, let's do that then.'

'OK. And what do you do for an occupation?'

I gesture towards my grey blazer.

'Ah, still a pupil at school?' She uncrosses her legs then crosses them again the other way. In the corner, a small fan sputters round. A very slight but quite irritating breeze hits me at the side of my face. Does she not see the weather outside today?

'When was the last time you had your period?'

'The tenth of August.'

'You know that for sure?'

'I put a star in my diary every month on the exact day it ends.'

'Oh, that's very organised.'

That's me. Organised. Not this person. Definitely not this person.

'It helps me to keep track.'

'And what was the date you were last active?'

'Well, I took a Pilates class a few weeks ago but I haven't gone back to my usual dance classes since I first found out.'

She smiles then clears her throat. 'No, I mean sexually active.'

'Oh, right.' My cheeks burn under this overhead lighting. Is it hot in here? Yes, it is, it's so hot in here. I'm now very grateful for that fan in the corner. 'Um…I'm not sure exactly, maybe late August before school started back?'

'But you're not sure?'

'No, not exactly.'

'OK. And was this your first time?'

I squirm under the weight of my jacket, feeling the fabric itch my arms. Why is it so damn hot in here? I turn my head to the door, wondering what that excited redhead is talking about with her nurse. Definitely not this. I doubt she had to answer questions like this. Firstly, she probably gave her real name and address, and also the nurse likely checked out that chunk of silver on her left ring finger.

'Stephanie?'

I turn back to her and bite my lip. 'No.'

Her eyebrows raise then fall quickly as she appears to compose herself. Her pen scratches away at the white paper on the clipboard.

Scratch.

Scratch.

'But I was in a serious relationship with that one. Very serious. We were going to get married…one day… maybe…at least I think we were.'

Scratch.

Scratch.

'We might still, you know.'

'And when did you take the pregnancy test?' she asks me, not glancing up.

'September. I made a note of the date right there. And it was positive. In fact, after the first one I took five more. And they all said positive.'

'One would have been sufficient.'

'No, I get that now,' I snip back.

'And if you're pregnant, will you tell the father?' She stops writing. 'Do you know who the father is?'

'Of course I know who the father is!'

She hovers her pen above the clipboard and sits back in her chair.

'Sorry. I mean, no, I haven't told him. Or anyone actually.'

'Do you plan to tell him?'

'I can't.'

'Why not?'

'I just can't.'

'OK,' she finally says. She lays the clipboard down on her desk and turns her chair back to me. 'And if you are pregnant what do you plan to do next?'

'Aren't you supposed to help me with that? This is the Family *Planning* Clinic. Isn't it your job to help me with a plan?'

The door knocks and another nurse appears from around the corner. She looks at me, in my uniform blazer, and her nose scrunches. She hands a vanilla-coloured envelope to Nurse Joanne then backs out of the room.

The nurse opens the folder and her eyes skim from left to right as she consumes the words. Then she closes it and attaches it to the back of her clipboard. 'Positive. You are pregnant. We can schedule an internal examination with the clinic doctor on staff here for next week, but what I suggest is that you consult with your usual doctor—'

'Pregnant?'

She cocks her head to the side. 'You knew this already.'

'I...I...' She's right, I knew this. I didn't need another test to confirm what I already knew, so why are my eyes watering? Why do I suddenly feel like I can't breathe? My throat is tight and painfully stretches across my chest. I rub my neck, like I'm being strangled by someone standing behind me.

She slides a jug of water closer to her and pours me a glass of water.

I tip the glass back and the water flushes the pain away. Slamming the glass back down on the wooden table, I clear my throat.

She raises an eyebrow and her brown-rimmed glasses

creep down her nose. 'Do you want to have this baby, Stephanie?'

Biting my lip, I gaze down at my thighs, the tight jean fabric stretching at the knees. I shake my head but don't say anything.

'OK,' she simply says.

'Is that…wrong?'

She slips the glasses off from the bridge of her nose and places them gently on the table. 'Believe me when I say that you're not the only one I've seen in here with an unwanted pregnancy.'

'Have they been as young as me?'

'Some of them.'

'Oh.' I'm tempted to ask if there would be anyone that I'd know, but I decide against it.

'Let's go over what that would look like. You'd schedule an appointment for an abortion—'

'An abortion?'

'Yes, that is what you're saying, right?'

'I guess so…I just…abortion? That word sounds so…final.'

'It kinda is. So you really have to be sure that's the road you want to go down.'

I can't see it any other way. I don't see myself pushing a pram down the street while my peers walk home from school, talking about the parties they'll go to at the weekend, the shops they bought their outfits from, even the plans they have for after graduation. I'll have no plans. The only life that awaits me after I finish high school is one filled with nappies, milk bottles, and a screaming baby that refuses to sleep. That is not my life. That is not me. I'm not ready for that. For this. 'Yeah, I'm sure.'

'So, let's schedule a time for you to come in and meet with a termination specialist.'

'Until then, how do I cover this up?'

'Loose fitting clothes. Excuse yourself from PE, avoid any strenuous physical activity, drink plenty of liquids and eat well. It's important to take care of yourself. Oh, and avoid alcohol and smoking. You know, just in case.'

'Just in case what? Because I won't be changing my mind.' I scoop up my belongings and head for the door.

'Oh, and Stephanie? If that is your real name, and it's OK if it's not—'

I grit my teeth and feel my eyes skim the floor. I hate lying.

'Reconsider talking to someone you're close to. This is a very important and difficult decision and whatever you decide you'll want someone there with you.'

Pressing down on the handle, the door pops open. Turning back, I meet her directly in the eyes. 'I don't have anyone to talk to. I'm on my own with this one.'

When I get outside, the cold air hits me like a train and I gasp for a breath. But it's not enough. I can't get enough air. I can't get far enough away from here. I start running down the street, further and further away from the doors of the clinic, from the future that awaits me. And I don't stop running.

My thighs ache, my feet pound the pavement hard. Then I remember what she said. I could keep running. Run so hard and so fast until this thing inside me dies. Then the decision would be made for me. I wouldn't have to do anything. It would be like destiny stepped in. Like I wasn't meant to have this baby. I wouldn't need to go through an abortion, risk having that information on my medical records, risk anyone knowing, anyone else judging me. It would be so easy. So easy to keep running, to keep going.

But I can't do it. I can't run. I won't run. My body won't let me. My legs stop and I collapse under the abrupt halt. And when I hit the ground, I start crying. I can't stop. Tears flow from my eyes, spilling down my cheeks, onto the hard pavement beneath my hands.

I'm so angry at myself.

I'm so sad at having to do this alone.

I'm so jealous of everyone who walks around me, so free, so unburdened.

I'm so…everything.

I curl up to my knees and scream into them, biting down a little on my thigh.

I hate everyone.

But mostly, I hate myself.

My phone vibrates in my coat pocket. I feel the reminder of the real world, everyone around me, against my leg.

I wipe my nose against the sleeve of my coat and yank out the phone. Comments, more comments, about my posts. More likes.

I feel sick. I'm disgusting. Everything I do hurts people. And I don't know why I keep doing it. Or maybe I do, and I don't want to admit it to myself.

I post comments about Trina so they don't find out.

I post comments about Sophia so they don't find out.

Because if everyone's looking at them, if everything's laughing at them, then they won't see me. They won't see the bump that's started growing above my jeans line. They won't see the shame I carry or hear the lies I tell. And if I keep pointing the finger at everyone else, keep the wheels turning on social media, keep the jeering at school, then I can keep the eyes off me, the finger off me. And I'll do anything for that. I'll go to any means. I will say anything, do anything. Because I'm not them. My face can't appear on the posts, my name can't be dragged into anything. No one can ever know that I am pregnant.

I will do whatever it takes to keep it that way.

And I will crush anyone who threatens that.

Anyone.

ULANA

Her hands slide up the nape of my neck and weave into my long thick hair. Hands like my own. Fingers a little longer than most women's. 'Piano hands.' That's what my dad calls them anyway. Thin, spindly digits that flicker and move fast and effortlessly across the keys. The same fingers that run through my hair now, twisting and looping up stray strands that tickle down my back. Her hands are soft, familiar. Her hands are my hands. Her flesh, her blood, her memories, they made me in every way. From my features to my love of literature and learning. My mother is an incredible woman. And as terrified as I am of upsetting my father, I am more afraid of disappointing my mother, which I know, deep down, would be impossible to do. My mother loves me. And I feel that love every day.

'Are you OK?' she asks me, as her hands divide my hair into three sections.

I nod and feel a gentle tug on my scalp as the sections are woven in and out into a tight braid.

'Is school going OK?'

I nod again, feeling the words stick in my throat. I want to tell her. I really do. But it wouldn't be fair to expect her to keep anything from my dad, her husband. And I'm not ready to tell him just yet. I may never be ready. But I'm running out of time.

'Mum, how old were you when you were introduced to Dad?'

Her pace quickens as she nears the end of the braid. 'I was eighteen years old.'

'That's only a year older than me,' I say, feeling my forehead tighten, like the braid down my spine.

'Morocco is a very different place to here,' she smiles. 'Eighteen means something different over there.'

'It means family? Not university?'

'Not necessarily. When we first met, your father made it very clear to me that he would support me if I wanted to pursue further education. I was very lucky to meet him. I almost didn't.'

'Why?'

'I didn't want to get married. I wanted to move away. I wanted to fall in love before marriage. I wanted a life that gave me some independence.'

'What happened?'

'Nothing happened. I got all that with your father.'

'But it was an arranged marriage,' I say slowly, feeling the unfamiliar words linger in my mouth.

'An arranged marriage isn't a forced marriage, Ulana. It's about two families bringing two people together who they believe will make each other very happy. Even married couples over here meet that way. It's not "arranged", sure, but often two people are brought together – "set up" – by their family or friends for the same reason. They plant a seed for love which continues to grow long after the wedding.'

'I never thought of it that way before.'

She smiles and ties a band around the bottom of my hair, securing the braid.

'Did you meet Dad before the wedding?'

'Of course. We met many times. Always in a group, but we had many conversations with each other. Long, meaningful conversations, which eventually led to love.'

'Was that allowed?'

'Of course. Like I said, nothing was forced upon us. We married because we wanted to.'

'But you dated first?'

She laughs and sprays a little hairspray around the hairline. 'Not dated. But yes, we spent some time together first.' She smooths the flyaways down with her fingers, those long spindly fingers that look like mine. She pulls my hijab up, tucks the fabric in with kirby grips and strokes my cheeks softly.

I open my mouth, feel my lips part. I'm going to tell her. She'd understand. She'd know why I waited this long to tell her about Aiden. She'd know why Aiden is in my life. She'd recognise the same love that she sought for herself when she was only a year older than I am today.

But I hesitate, just for a second. One second. And the moment passes.

As she walks away, her back to me, hairspray and brush still in her hands, warm tears prick the corners of my eye. And I refrain from screaming her name, calling her back to me, back to the truth.

I want to tell her about Sunday. I try to, more than once. But Sunday rolls around fast. Too fast. And then it's too late.

While my dad prepares to go to the mosque in Glasgow for Zuhr, the second prayer of the day, I prepare my lies for the day.

'You sure you don't want me to come with you?' I ask him, as he zips up his coat. Soft misty rain trickles down from heavy dark clouds above.

'No, you enjoy the afternoon with your friend. I like her.' He smiles. He gently touches a hand to my cheek then starts checking all the switches in the kitchen. He's always done that since I was little. He's terrified of fire, so he checks and rechecks that everything is switched off and unplugged. I always remind him that the houses here are packed so tightly together that if next door is

on fire, chances are we'd be next despite our strenuous safety measures. But he doesn't listen. He just checks and rechecks. I slide off the seat and unplug the kettle and toaster for him.

I check my watch. Sophia's late. What if she doesn't come? 'You should head out. You can't be late.'

'I'll wait until Sophia comes. Then I know you're safe. I don't want you walking there alone.'

'I think she's running late, Dad.'

'Then I'll walk you myself.'

Hurry up, Sophia!

The doorbell rings and a loud sigh escapes my lungs. I slide off the chair and rush to the door before my dad even turns around.

Sophia stands on the other side, hair damp from the misty rain, skin pale, cheeks hollow. She tries to smile, but it looks too painful for her.

'Hi,' I whisper. 'Thanks for coming.'

My dad comes up behind me. 'Hello, Sophia!'

She tries again at smiling. No success.

'You don't look so good? Are you feeling ill?' he asks her.

'I'm fine. I'm just recovering from a cold. But I'm much better,' she lies, convincingly.

'Well, we'd better get going,' I interrupt before the conversation goes any further. I know her mind is bogged with Steve thoughts and I can't risk a slip up. 'Lunch will be ready soon and we can't keep Sophia's parents waiting.'

'Should I pick you up later?'

'No!' I yell at my dad. I clear my throat and try not to glance at Sophia. 'I mean, I'm not sure what time lunch will be finished and I don't want to rush them. Sophia will walk me home, or her parents will give me a lift. Right?'

Sophia simply nods. Right, it's time for us to leave. This could go wrong quickly. 'Bye Dad!'

I nudge her away from the door, and loop my arm between hers, dragging her down the road. I glance back and smile at my dad who's still standing at the door waving at us. A deep sensation burns at the bottom of my belly. Guilt? Shame? Regret?

Why did I say yes to this?

'Sorry. I hope I didn't mess it up for you back there,' she mutters, her voice barely audible. A damp piece of hair falls across her face and sticks to her rain-slicked cheek. She doesn't brush it away. She doesn't even seem to feel it. Or feel anything at all right now actually.

'No, you were great. Thanks for coming. Sorry to drag you out. I know you have other things going on. Speaking of, have you heard from Steve?'

'Nothing. Not one text. Not one response to any of mine either.'

'You texted him?'

'Of course. I asked him to take the photos down and he just ignored me.'

'They're still up?' I gasp.

'Yes. I'm going to report him on Facebook.'

'Why haven't you done that yet?'

'Because he'll get banned and I'm scared that'll draw more attention to the photos. Plus what if Facebook contacts the police because of my age and they get involved, then the school finds out, my parents find out. That's going to be more humiliating. If it can even get any worse that is.'

We walk a little faster, through the park, past the slides, around the fence, behind a set of old council estate houses.

'That's Trina Davis' house,' I point out.

A little rabbit hutch sits in the back garden, the animal having long since died. The wood looks soft in the rain, and the metal grid on the gate looks rusted.

'I always forget that you were friends with Trina Davis.'

'Yeah, I guess we were,' I shrug. It all seems so long ago now. Those days where everything seemed so easy, and everyone just got along with everyone. There were no cliques, no rules, no gossiping, no bullying, no writing of names on bathroom doors, no social media shaming. Everything was just so innocent back then. So different. A world I can barely remember now. And what about the generation that comes after me? What legacy are we leaving for them if I can barely remember a time before social media?

'What was she like?'

'Hmm?'

'Trina. What was she like back then when you were friends with her?'

'She was different from how she is now. My parents would never let me hang out with her now if they knew her reputation. Reputation is everything to them. If they knew what people say about her, they'd worry that I'd be tarnished with the same bad brush. Is that the saying?'

'You, tarnished? Yeah right.'

'Yeah, but I couldn't risk it. I still see her at school obviously. But we don't really talk much. Maybe a quick "Hi" in the hallway if we pass, which we don't really. We take different classes. But I feel bad for her. Especially now. She looks like she's been having a hard time. She looks like she's been crying every time I see her.'

'Yeah, Lucy McNeil makes everyone's life a living hell.' Sophia rubs away a tear with the heel of her hand, then looks away.

'I'm sorry that—'

'Don't worry. I'll be fine. We're here.'

I resist pulling her in for a hug, knowing that she might crumble in my arms. So I keep my hands down by my hips and turn away. Aiden's house is bigger than I expected. Much bigger. A tall iron gate encircles a large rectangular white stone house, with a conservatory that juts out on the right, topped with a smaller version of a turret. In the front garden, scattered among the crushed copper stones, sit heavy ceramic plant pots with tall green leaves sticking out, some flopping over onto the stones. A black Range Rover is parked in front of a double garage door, painted copper like the stones. A white cat lays out on the damp step by the main door, head half resting on the welcome mat.

'Well?'

'Well,' I say. I take a deep breath. 'OK, here goes.' I push open the gate, and swing it back around, sealing myself inside the garden. 'Thanks again, Sophia.'

She tries that smile again, then turns to leave, the heavy mist encasing her, taking her from me. Then she's gone.

When I turn around, Aiden's face appears in the living room window and I instantly feel my heartbeat slow down. The door swings open and the cat meows loudly, momentarily annoyed at being disturbed, then scampers inside back into the dry warmth.

'Hi.' He's beaming from ear to ear.

'Hi.' My cheeks hurt so I must be doing the same. I pass through the entrance, giving Aiden a quick kiss on the cheek.

He takes my hand and leads me into the kitchen. Standing by the oven, spatula in hand, surrounded by a ceiling of pots and pans, and an island counter as big as my bed, is a beautiful woman with coppery blonde hair that bounces right above her shoulder bones. She vigorously stirs a ceramic bowl filled with what looks like flour and butter, and then glances up.

A big smile pulls tight across my face. Then I see hers.

She looks…surprised. Then she shakes her head and a smile suddenly appears. 'Hi, you must be Ulana. Aiden doesn't stop talking about you.' She rushes over to shake my hand but stops only inches from me. 'Sorry, am I allowed to…'

I reach my hand out and take hers. 'It's nice to meet you finally.'

'Is that the elusive Ulana I hear?' Aiden's dad rushes through, beer in one hand, remote control in the other. He stops at the steps of the kitchen, glances at me then his wife, then moves into the space, smiling. 'It's nice to meet you.' He raises his arms to hug me, then quickly draws it back.

'It's nice to meet you too,' I mutter. I realise I've taken my shoes off at the door and while I stand in their beautiful big kitchen in green polka dot socks, they all have their shoes on. In fact, I couldn't look more different from these people if I tried to. I suddenly don't feel so good. 'Excuse me, where's your bathroom?'

'I'll show you.' Aiden nudges me out the door, taking my hand again. 'It's right there.'

He starts up the stairs.

'Where are you going?' I blurt out, rushing out of the bathroom.

'I'll be right down. Relax. They won't bite.'

I linger in the bathroom, splashing cold water on my face. Then I adjust my hijab and pinch my cheeks to bring a little colour to the surface. I turn off the light and creep out into the carpeted hallway. My socks really pop against the beige. In fact everything in this house is beige. Except me.

I hear their whispers from the kitchen before they hear my footsteps. I don't hear Aiden, only his parents. I wait by the kitchen wall and listen in, just for a few seconds.

'He did say her parents were "strict", that's why we hadn't met her before today.'

'He didn't say she was...she was...'

'Muslim?'

'How is this going to work? They're so different from each other.'

'Maybe that's why he likes her. She seems sweet.'

'And I'm sure she is. But she's Muslim. We're Catholic. They're not like us, Ed.'

'They'? Does she mean me? My family? Or my whole community?

My ears warm and I feel nauseous again. I hear Aiden moving around upstairs, but suddenly he's not familiar to me anymore. Nothing here is.

My feet walk back to the bathroom, and I turn the light on again and stand at the mirror. My eyes are watering at the edges and my cheeks are starting to redden. Maybe I shouldn't have taken off my shoes. Maybe I should have snuck a little more make-up on. But, who am I kidding? Lip gloss and mascara wouldn't have made me look any different. Because that's what I'm feeling right now and that's what they're seeing. That's what they think I am.

Different.

TRINA

<u>(Not answering the door to anyone tonight – It's Not
Safe – nowhere is anymore)</u>

The best thing happened to me this week. I'd been pray-
ing for a way to get Lucy McNeil back for everything she's
put me through. And my prayers were finally answered.
Finally a step in my direction, a win for my team.

So this is amazing. Let's just emphasise how much
Lucy portrays herself as Little Miss Perfect (I'll call her
LMP)–she always looks like she's spent about two hours
washing, blow-drying, straightening then tonging her
hair every single morning. Also, who goes to all that
effort to style their hair until it looks pin straight then
goes and takes a heated curler to it? <u>Counter</u> <u>Productive</u>!
There's a big word for her!

Anyway, back to her hair – it's not too straight to be lank, but not too tonged to be curled. OK, even though I hate her, she does rock some good celebrity hair in the mornings. BUT, it's all a front. Like everything else on her body and in her life, generally. More on that after.

Now her make-up: pinched cheeks, contoured cheekbones, dark mascara-brushed eyebrows that look like they've been tattooed on (have they?), highlighted collarbone and lip gloss that looks like it costs more than my mum's car. A bit boring on the make-up side for me. She's not going to church. Ha! That's the last place she's going, but we'll get to that.

Nails? Either a French manicure or a dusty rose shade. Gels. Always gels. LMP doesn't have time for a chip.

She almost never wears the same outfit twice. Her family clearly have money to burn. She's always going on about the holidays her dad takes her and her mum on. Whoopee! She's rich! Who cares? Let's talk about the fact that those expensive jeans she slides into every morning are no longer fitting her! Yes, that's way more exciting.

You know, I was thinking before this happened that LMP was looking a little 'fuller' these days, especially around the hips and chest, but I thought she'd just eased up her crazy diets. Oh, if you thought her skinny figure was a blessing from Mother Nature, think again. Prior to the last few weeks, the most I've seen that girl eat is a whole banana. But here she is 'randomly' gaining weight (but also not random at all!). Even her hair is looking a little dishevelled these days. And her skin? It's looking a bit grey if you ask me…OK, no one is, but I'm still going to mention it because she deserves it. Any ten of my posts don't touch even one of her posts. She's lethal with her words. I just tell the truth. And that's exactly what I did today. Tell the truth. To everyone.

I'm getting ahead of my myself.

Let's start from the beginning:

Actually, side note: I've decided that instead of LMP, I'm going to refer to her from now on as LMH – Little Miss Hypocrite! Because that's what she is: a lying, pathetic hypocrite! And I'm exposing her for just that. It's not mean. It's not revenge. It's justice. Sophia would understand if I asked her. See, I'm not the only one who's been having the worst school year ever because of her. Lucy bullies everyone and loves to point out everyone's faults, and then laughs at them. Well, not anymore. This time the tables are being turned on her. This time she finally gets what's been coming to her for years. Gone will be her little admirers and followers, gone is that perfect hair, those perfect nails, those perfectly fitting outfits, that perfect make-up. No, there will be nothing perfect about her anymore.

It's going to be hard to find the time (and the energy I heard, but I wouldn't know!) to get manicures, go shopping, spend hours in front of the mirror doing her hair

– straighten, curl, straighten, curl – even catching up on gossips with her army followers will be hard. Because –

Because –

Because –

Are you ready? –

LUCY MCNEIL IS

PREGNANT!!

PREGNANT??

PREGNANT!!!!

Yep, I saw her leaving the Family Planning Clinic in town and now that I look at her, she is without a doubt rounder in the belly. Considering this girl's hip bones jutted out like a coat rack, any bump would be obvious to anyone. But no one is looking for a baby bump. I wasn't. Until I saw her rush out those clinic doors, leaflets in hand, splotchy red face like she'd been crying.

Yes, that girl is having a baby.

And I would bet my life on it that it isn't Rhys'.

Look, I'm not the bully here, she is! She hurts people all the time. She hurt me. She spread lies about what happened at the party. She hurt Sophia. And yesterday I saw her being bitchy to a poor Fifth Year! I just wanted to give her a taste of her own medicine. So, I took a photo of her leaving the Family Planning Clinic and posted it for everyone to see. I even tagged Rhys in it too, just to make sure he knows the truth. I captioned it:

'LUCY MCNEIL IS PREGNANT AND DOESN'T KNOW WHO THE FATHER IS!!'

OK, I did feel a <u>little</u> guilty after I hit Post, but now I don't. I didn't deserve any of the abuse I got online for something that I didn't ask for. What happened to me happened against my will, and I was scared. I felt so low. I wanted to die. And Lucy made it so much worse by laughing about it online, and posting rumours about it for everyone to see. It was like what happened to me at the party was happening all over again. Like I was being taken advantage of all over again, like I was saying no again but no one was listening, like I was screaming for help – and again, no one came.

I don't feel bad at all.

Not one bit.

If I could, I'd post that photo all over again. This time, I'd tag everyone she knows, everyone she ever knew – her parents, relatives, neighbours, even her priest if she had one (and if he had a Facebook account too, obviously).

I must be getting to her because she wasn't in school today. And I'd bet anything that she won't be in school tomorrow or the day after that. She's ashamed! And she should be. What's that saying, that people in glass houses shouldn't throw stones?

Well, I'm breaking down Lucy's glass house – or should I say her glass palace. Yep, it's all coming down. And I can't wait to watch that girl suffer.

Like I said she deserves this…

Doesn't she?

Yes she does – I think – so why do I suddenly feel really sick about all this?

SOPHIA

I cross my legs. Then uncross them. Then cross again.

Beside me, my dad's knee bounces up and down. His fingers grip the upholstery on the arms of the chair he slouches in, ankle perched over thigh. His jaw is clenched and he faces straight ahead. He hasn't looked at me once since we got here. I'm not surprised. I can't look at myself either. The mirrors in my bedroom are swathed in pashminas and silk scarves. Anything to keep them from revealing what I fear the most these days. Me. My reflection.

My mum sits on my left. Her back is so straight, her spine naturally sits away from the back of the chair. Her vertebrae hasn't touched the cheap upholstery once. Her quilted leather handbag sits beside her feet, which are squeezed into black pumps. Her hand grips the leather strap as if Headmaster Tomlinson might steal it. Or maybe she's keeping it from my fingers.

I'm unpredictable these days.

Like an animal in the wild: 'Approach with Caution'.

My mum rubs her neck with a wide open palm. I'm glad to see I'm not the only one wishing I was a million miles from this room.

Finally, the headmaster enters from behind our chairs. The door slams shut and my mum's back arches as if she's still trying to escape the fabric of the chair.

Tomlinson plops down into the leather chair at his desk, the base swivelling his body away from us. He returns it to face us then leans in, planting his elbows on the table to stabilise himself. He takes a deep loud breath and passes a slow look between each of us. When it's my turn, I can't hold his gaze so I look down at my mum's tapping feet.

'Mr Greer. Mrs Greer. Sophia. Sorry to keep you all waiting. I'm afraid I'm still dealing with this…*incident*. We're still finding more posters. This time behind the chemistry labs.'

My dad clears my throat and we think he's going to speak, finally, so we turn to face him. But he doesn't. My mother rolls her eyes and leans in, further away from the spine of the chair that disgusts her. 'I'm still trying to figure out how these photos of my daughter appeared in the first place? Who took them?'

Headmaster Tomlinson glances at me and waits for me to respond to that one.

Nope. No thanks.

'Well, Mrs Greer. It seems that the person had these photos on his phone and either passed them along to his friends or printed them himself. And now these posters are everywhere.'

In the hallways. In the study hall. In the cafeteria. On the toilet cubicles. Boys' and girls'. On the blackboard in my Attendance Room. Hung on door handles. Taped on whitewash walls. Glued onto classroom desks. Everywhere. No inch of this school building was left untainted, unspoiled, by my naked body.

'Who did it?' she asks.

'We don't know exactly. There are several people involved in this—'

'But who had the original photos to begin with?' Mum won't let this one go that easily.

'Steven Gordon.'

And there it is.

My dad squeezes his temples with his index finger and thumb, and painfully scrunches his face. He gets it. He knows. Daddy's little girl. Not anymore.

'Steve?' My mum clearly still isn't getting it. 'Why would Steve do this? Why would he have these photos…' Her eyes burn into the side of my face as I desperately stare into the legs of the desk. 'Oh…right. I see.'

Now she gets it.

'Sophia,' she whispers. Actually it's more of a gasp than

a whisper. A disappointed, horrified gasp. Then she turns to Tomlinson, her cheeks reddening, her jaw tighter than I've ever seen it. 'Why aren't Steve's parents here too? This involves him and them too. More importantly, has he been expelled for this?'

'We are meeting with him and his parents later this week. I can't divulge too much information as to the consequences for him but I assure you—'

'So he's still attending school here, like normal?'

'Well, yes he's—'

'Why is it that my daughter is the one sitting here like she's being punished for this while he continues to attend school and be with his friends like nothing happened?' She's yelling now. Loudly. I can hear whispering outside the door, the office secretary maybe. 'I want that boy expelled immediately! In fact, I'm going to call his mother right now.' She and I lunge for her handbag at the same time.

'No, Mum! Stop, please don't call them!' I wrestle with her fingers, pulling the zip back in place as she forces it open. This will make it worse. They don't understand how embarrassed I already am. I can't take any more.

Tomlinson claps his hands together and my dad startles and slides down another inch in his chair. 'Please, Mrs Greer, Sophia. This isn't helping the situation. We should just discuss how to move forward with this.'

My mum stops, her fingers hovering above the bag, zip half open. 'What do you mean?' she asks.

'Well, if Sophia wants to take some time off, we can certainly organise that. It's clearly causing her some discomfort and humiliation, which is understandable. She can afford the time to spend time at home, rest, regroup, and—'

My mum frantically waves her hand in front of him. 'She can't afford to take time off this year. She's graduating soon and going to university.'

'I'm sorry, Mrs Greer, but it's unlikely that Sophia will be graduating this year with her current grades if she intends to go to university in September.'

'What?' My mum's voice echoes around the room. Outside, passing cars and screams of teenagers hanging out at the park opposite compete for my attention. And clearly my dad's. And I thought *I* was uncomfortable sitting here.

'Sophia's attendance has fallen below forty per cent. We've had to contact the council's education welfare officer. Since she is over 16, there's nothing formally that can be done but right now she does not have the academic profile to graduate. And it's unlikely that she'll pass her Highers this term if her preliminary exam scores are anything to go by. You should be prepared for another year at Birchwood to secure the grades required by... where did you apply, Sophia?'

'Newcastle,' I stutter, the sounds trembling on my lips.

'Newcastle?' my mum echoes. 'I didn't know you had applied there. Why Newcastle, it's so far away?'

Steve applied there, so I did. I didn't want to be too far from him. I can't tell my parents that though, not now. They wouldn't understand. No one ever does.

'Well, with some tutoring—'

'How are we just hearing about this now?'

'The school has sent notices home, Mrs Greer,' Tomlinson sighs. He picks up his ballpoint pen and drops it down on a file. My file.

'We didn't receive anything in the post?' She slowly turns to look at me. 'Did you hide these letters from the school?' she asks me.

A deep breath escapes my throat and I look beyond Tomlinson's head, into the park ahead, wishing I was there with them. Soaring high on the swings they lean against, chatting, laughing, joking. But I'm not. I'm here. And here, I'm invisible. Just a name on a file. A name in an 'incident'. A disappointment to my parents.

'I didn't know what to tell you,' I finally say, but it comes out more like a strained whisper.

'The truth for a start!'

'Mrs Greer—'

'Thank you, Mr Tomlinson, for your time and for your swift handling of this "incident". We'll take it from here.' She stands and heavily gestures to Dad and I to do the same. We stumble to our feet and start gathering up our coats. I swing my bag up over my shoulder, once heavy but now light with a lack of textbooks and apparently an empty future. I don't look back at Tomlinson before I close his door shut.

Our feet slap the cold hard tiles as she leads us to the side exit that spills out onto the rear car park. The cool early November air slaps at our cheeks and blows our collars as we hurry to the car. Mum doesn't say a word to us until we're inside.

'I just can't believe all this, Sophia. What were you thinking? Sending those photos to Steve? No…wait, taking those photos at all? I don't get it! Why?'

'Everyone else is doing it!' I argue, struggling with the clip on my belt.

'I don't care what everyone else is doing. I only care about what my own daughter is doing. Under my roof, might I add! And now look what's happened?'

'Mae—'

'Don't start, James. You didn't say a word during that entire meeting. You may as well have not come!'

'Mum, I—'

'And your attendance? Your grades? Hiding mail?'

'She's clearly been distracted—'

'James, this is serious. I'm furious that we're just learning of all this now. I'll be sending Headmaster Tomlinson a letter first thing tomorrow morning. I want that boy off school grounds. In the meantime, we'll get her enrolled for next year and focus on bringing her grades back up and—'

'I can't go back to Birchwood, Mum,' I gasp. 'I'll repeat my last year anywhere else, I'll leave and get a job, I'll take an access course at the local college, I'll do home schooling. Anything. But I'm not going back there!'

'This isn't your decision, Sophia. You've already proved you can't make mature or appropriate decisions for yourself.'

'Mum, I said I was sorry! I made a mistake! You can't make me spend another year at that school! Everyone knows—'

'And they're all leaving this year. They'll pass their exams and have a place at a university, unlike you.'

'But what about the year below? And even the year below that. Everyone at Birchwood knows what happened. It doesn't matter what class they put me in, people will know what happened. They'll know my name.'

'You should have thought of that before you sent those photos. Before you started skipping classes and missing assignments.'

'Mae—'

'James, you've babied her for too long.'

'*I've* babied her? You've sheltered her too and now look what's happened. And Steve? You know I never liked him from the start. You're the one who encouraged that relationship.'

'Maybe if you didn't work all the time, you would have—'

'Maybe if you didn't spend so much money on frivolous purchases and overpriced holidays I wouldn't have to work so much!'

I cover my face with my hands. 'Stop fighting,' I say as their voices get louder, angrier.

'And who was it that said she was too young to get her own phone? I said I didn't want her with a phone until she went to uni, but you went out and bought her one!'

'All of her friends have one!'

'Sophia, are all of your friends doing this too? Ulana? Did Ulana know about this?'

'Of course not!' I cry from the back. This car is so full, so full with anger, with confusion, with hate. Make it stop.

My mum continues, as if I'm not there behind them, as if my feelings don't matter. As if I'm invisible again.

'Stop fighting, please,' I beg.

They don't hear me.

They don't know I'm even there.

No one does.

I fumble with the belt again, this time to undo it. Their voices are so loud now. They scream at each other, blaming each other for my actions. They're still yelling when I open the car door and run out.

My feet pound the empty car park as I run away from the car, from the school, from the park out front, from the swings. From everything.

I don't stop running until a branch whips at my face, bringing me to. When I look around, I realise I've run deep into the woods behind the school. Leaves gather around my boots. Mud sits on the toe of one of them.

My fingers search for my phone in my coat pocket, and I yank it out. Four texts from Ulana.

Did Steve put up those posters of you?!

Just found more in the girls' toilets. I'm going to kill him!!

Are you OK, Sophia?

I heard your parents have to come in to see Tomlinson. Sorry :(

My thumbs press into the screen as I frantically smash out a message. But it's not to Ulana.

Steve – can we talk? Please. I can't take this anymore. Please stop doing this. I'm sorry. I'm so sorry.

LUCY

Their whispers follow me down the hallway. Their heads turn when I pass. Their eyes drop down when I turn to face them. I float through the halls like I'm dreaming. Bodies skim my shoulder but I'm numb to their touch. I move in slow motion while those around me are stuck in a movie, succumbing to the fast-forward button. It's like that dream where no matter how fast you move, how far you travel, you can never reach your destination. You're just short of making it to the end. And just when you think you're going to succeed, just when you think you're almost there, you wake up. That's me. I've just woken up. But not from a dream. No. This is a nightmare.

Rage courses through me like I've never felt before. My body is on fire. I hate her. And not the kind of hate someone carries for a short time before they forget all about it because they believe life to be too short to hold grudges. No. I HATE her. The kind of hate I have with me right now is the kind that will last forever because it's fuelled from deep within, from a place that I hope never experiences hatred like this again.

I don't want her to die. That would be too easy. I want Trina Davis to suffer. I want her to suffer so much that she begs me to stop. And I won't. Not ever.

It's only a matter of time before my parents find out from social media that their seventeen-year-old daughter is pregnant...*was* pregnant. Because at that point, the... It...will be terminated, and I can go back to living my normal life as it was before this.

But can I?

Lily barely looked at me in Attendance today and left me to walk to class by myself for the first time ever. I never walk through these halls alone. I always have my friends by my side, attached to my hip, some might even say. But not today. Today I walk alone. And this is Trina's doing.

My hands tremble as I reach the big grey doors of the cafeteria. This is ridiculous. This is *my* school. *My* cafeteria. No one makes me feel like this. Especially not her. I take a deep breath, letting the air fill my lungs and expand my chest, and push the doors open.

Faces turn to watch me as I push through the crowd, whispers, eyes, even the odd smirk. Then I don't have to struggle through anymore, because the crowd parts for me. My heart beats wildly. I'm an animal at the zoo.

Spectators circle around me, pointing, marvelling at the animal, once free and untamed, that stands here submissively, tail between legs.

I find Cara, Lily, Mollie and Lee sitting at our table in the back. They already have their lunch trays, but no one is eating. They huddle together looking at Lee's phone screen. Cara glances up and sees me. She elbows Lee and he promptly slides his phone into his coat pocket.

'Hey,' I say, inching towards the chair that I always sit in.

'Um, hey,' Lee replies.

Lily waves. Cara does her fake half smile. And Mollie just stares at Lily and Cara, wondering what her greeting should be. In the end, she does nothing, she just goes back to dunking her carrots in her hummus dip.

My body edges into the chair but I sit forward, in case I need to stand quickly. 'What's going on?' My voice sounds too high. Too weak. They'll see right through me.

Lily shrugs. 'Not much.'

'Anything you want to tell us?' Cara leans into the table, closer to me.

Here we go. 'I suppose you've seen Trina's Facebook posts and that's what this is all about? Well, none if it is true.'

'Really?' Lily shakes her head. 'Because there were photos of you leaving the clinic. And, well, now that she mentions it, you do look a little…a little…'

'A little what?' I snap.

'Rounder,' Mollie shrugs, a carrot dropping from her fingers onto the table. She picks it up, blows off any potential dirt from the sticky tray, then dunks it into the tub of hummus beside her.

'I'm not pregnant!'

People turn to locate the drama and immediately spot me at the centre. They shuffle closer, leaning in, straining to hear all the juicy details.

'You definitely look like you're pregnant,' Lee says.

My cheeks are warm and my mouth suddenly feels dry. My tongue sticks to the sides of my mouth, desperate for moisture.

'If it's not true then why were you at the Family Planning Clinic? And why didn't you tell us? Aren't we your best friends? Do you know what it feels like to find this out over social media?' asks Cara.

'I wasn't at the Family Planning Clinic. Trina obviously followed me, and then took a photo of me walking past it. I was outside it – not inside it. This is all part of her tricks. She's just playing all of you—'

'Sounds like a lot of excuses, if you ask me,' Lily mutters loudly.

'Well, no one is asking you!' I've had enough. I'm not sitting through one more question. I push back my chair until it hits the wall behind me. When I turn to storm out, I bump into Euan and Steve. Steve smirks at me, so I put my hands up and shove him hard. But not hard enough.

'Whooa!' he laughs, stumbling back into a chair. 'Somebody's hormones are out of control!'

Euan jumps to my side and dramatically pretends to part the crowd. 'Baby coming through, move out the way! Baby coming through!'

A large group of people erupt in laughter, a few others cover their mouths, too shocked to respond any other way. Past the crowd, beyond the taunts, the jeers, the jibes, I see Ulana. She holds the cafeteria door open and waves me over. I see my exit. My escape. Swiping my arms, I propel myself forward towards her. She stands to the side of the doorframe, and ushers me through to safety. I hesitate at the doorway, knowing I should thank her, or at the very least apologise for talking about her behind her back, or for posting comments about her best friend online. But the words 'I'm sorry' get stuck in my throat, unfamiliar and foreign to me. So I push past her also and hurl my body down the hall and out the main door.

I hear the school receptionist calling my name, asking me to come back. But I don't turn back. I can't. I know exactly where I'm going.

It's not the second bell yet. I know exactly where Trina Davis will be right now.

I cut through the woods to loop around the building.

Mud kicks up around my ankle boots, staining the yet untreated beige suede, but I don't care. Low hanging branches scratch at my face, autumn leaves still hanging on dotted with amber flecks. A light rain falls softly around me and catches in my long hair. The cold cuts right through me. Tiny goose bumps spread all over my bare legs. My black pleated skirt lifts and flaps slightly in the wind. The trail forks, the left going up, deeper into the woods, away from prying eyes, while the right goes down the hill and spills out into the alleyway at the back of the building.

I find her exactly where I knew she'd be. Standing in the alleyway behind the chemistry labs, cigarette in hand. She smokes beside another girl. But when she sees me, she elbows Trina and then rushes off, away from the volcano about to erupt.

I grab Trina before she's even turned around and shake her wildly. Her cigarette drops to the ground by her feet, and her shoulder bag slips off and catches at her wrist. I end the shaking with a heavy shove and see her collapse down on the ground. She looks different today. Gone is the short skirt, V-neck top too low. Today she wears a baggy school jumper, frayed at the sleeves, and a pair of black ripped jeans. Even her make-up is gone.

Another girl leans against the wall, pulls out a cigarette box and slides another out. She rummages around for a lighter.

'Do you want to be next?!' I scream at her.

The cigarette drops from her agape mouth.

'Then go inside!'

She fumbles for her bag strap, grips it in her palm, and rushes down the alleyway towards the door. I don't need another audience. This is between me and Trina, no one else. This ends today.

When I turn back, Trina is on her feet again, smoothing down her too-long jumper, which is now muddy and wet from the puddle where she landed.

I run at her again and push myself into her. She wriggles out from my grasp, but doesn't touch me. My hand grips onto her wrist as I pull myself up. My elbow collides with her ribs, and she groans and staggers back. But again she doesn't touch me, or reach for me, or fight back in any way.

'I'm not fighting you.'

'Too scared?' I say, running at her again.

She shifts out of the way but grabs my arm to steady me so I don't hit the wall. I shoulder her off me. Face damp from the rain and sweat, I stop to catch my breath. Why won't she fight me? My chest heaves in and out, rising up and out then falling heavily.

She grabs her bag and heads up the trail, deeper into the woods.

'Don't you dare walk away from me!' I follow her, but her steps are faster than mine. 'Hey!' I walk faster, then start jogging a little. 'I'm not finished yet!'

'Go away!' she yells, without slowing down or turning back.

'No! I'm not going anywhere! Do you have any idea what you did to me in there?'

'Nothing worse than what you've done to me!'

Her steps quicken and I fumble on the path, trying to keep up.

'You posted a photo of me coming out of the Family Planning Clinic! Everyone saw!'

'You spread rumours about me from Lee's party! Everyone called me a slut! You wrote my name on the toilet cubicles, you even posted a photo of me drunk from the party implying that I was asking for it!'

'You were! I only told the truth!'

She spins round, her eyes wild. 'You don't know anything about the truth! You have no idea what happened at that party!'

'Everyone knows what happened at that party!'

'You only think you know what happened. But you're wrong. I didn't want that to happen. I didn't say that it was OK! I said no to him and he forced me!'

'What are you saying?' I ask, moving closer to her.

She tucks one side of her hair behind her ear, exposing four different piercings along the lobe. One earring has a pink stone, while another is a silver bar that pops out at an awkward angle. 'Forget it. Just forget I said anything.' She marches ahead, leaving me to chase after her again.

'You're lying! You're just saying that to play the victim because—'

'Don't you dare call me a victim!' she screams behind her, tossing the words into the rain and letting them hit me. 'You wouldn't understand, and you certainly don't care. All you care about is yourself.' She turns and stands tall on a raised lip in the trail. 'You're a selfish, pathetic—'

A deep groan escapes my mouth, as I grip the trunk of a tree beside me to steady my balance.

'Lucy?'

My hand hurts from pressing into the bark so hard. Sharp splinters dig into my palm, but I don't let go. It hurts too much. My chest tightens and I struggle to fill my lungs with air. Sharp pain explodes low in my belly. I grit my teeth and lean over. The pain. It's too much.

Trina is suddenly standing over me, her hand on my shoulder. 'Lucy?'

I open my mouth to tell her to leave me alone, but the words don't flow out. They get stamped out by the scream I never felt coming.

The pain.

It's too much. It's too…

Please stop the pain.

'What should I do?' She sounds panicked. Scared. Lost. 'Lucy, what should I do? I don't know what to do?' She's crying. Or is it me? Are those my tears?

'I'm going to get help!'

'No!' I grab her wrist and pull her close to me. I'm on my knees, huddled into a ball. There's blood. My blood. I'm bleeding. 'Don't…please…' I spit and splutter with the words.

'What? Tell me?'

'Don't leave me!' I scream out, as the pain rips through my middle.

'OK. OK.' She pulls out her phone but I don't know who she's calling. Her words are muffled, panicked bursts of half-formed sentences and scrambled rants. She tosses her phone on the ground by my bag and drops to her knees beside me. 'Help's coming.'

'Don't leave me,' I say again as I fold into her arms, still tucked into a ball.

She cradles my head. 'I'm not leaving, I promise.' Her hands brush the hair from my face, and gently she strokes the strands. 'I won't leave you, Lucy.'

'Trina, I—'

'Shh. Don't say anything. It's OK. I'm right here.'

It's so hot out here. My body is on fire. Every part of me burns with searing hot pain. My eyelids are suddenly heavy. Fatigue sweeps over me like a wave and takes me in its grip. The last thing I see before darkness takes me is Trina's face. The last thing I hear are her words, gentle and soothing.

ULANA

I stand, facing the toilet door.

My body is burning inside.

A flutter circles inside my belly and moves up to my chest, through the rib cage, up my throat, and settles in my jaw. I clench my teeth so hard they could break inside my mouth.

I've never felt anger like this before. My fingers tingle. I want to hit something. I want to hit someone. No, not just anyone. I want to hit Steve.

I snatch up my bag and hurl the toilet door open, letting it bang against the wall. Then I walk out, not even stopping to wash my hands. This needs to be said. Now.

The words on the toilet door float fresh in my mind, hovering at the forefront, refusing to be pushed to the side. Refusing to be accepted, to be forgotten about.

SOPHIA GREER LOVES TO POSE IN HER
UNDERWEAR!

CHECK OUT THE NUDE PICS ON FACEBOOK!!

I push my way through the lunch crowd, and find Cara, Lily, Euan and Lee sitting at the big round table in the back. Before I can think about what to say, I put my hand on Cara's chair, 'Where's Steve?'

They all turn to face me.

'Steve?' I ask again.

Euan shrugs and looks around the table at everyone else's reactions.

'Did he write that on the toilet door about Sophia? Or was it one of you?'

Cara sits back in the chair, her tray of lunch untouched in front of her. 'What are you talking about?'

I place a hand on their table and lean in to her. 'You know exactly what I'm talking about.'

She shrugs and slides her salad tray away. A piece of lettuce spills out from the plastic bowl onto the red tray. 'Well, what did it say?' she asks.

'It said…um…it—'

'Aw, she can't even say it,' chimes in Lily, gesturing to me like I'm a piece in the game they're playing, only they didn't ask me first whether I wanted to join. I didn't. I don't like games. I don't have time for games.

'You know what it says. Who wrote it?' I ask them again.

Cara stands to face me, her long lithe body unfolding

from the chair. Her shoulders sit taller than mine, and she knows this. 'If you have something to say to us then just say it, Ulana.'

I don't move my hand. I don't take a step back. 'Yeah, I do actually. All this needs to stop. She doesn't deserve this, or Trina Davis.'

'Steve told us Sophia posted those photos of herself, and then changed her mind and blamed him,' Lily says. 'Besides, most of those comments came from Lucy so take it up with her.'

'I will, but I'm taking it up with all of you. And Steve's lying. I'm going to say this one last time, this stops or I go to the Headmaster and file a bullying report. You can kiss your Prefect badges goodbye. And then I will pay all of your parents a visit too.'

Cara moves closer to me. She stands only inches from my face. She leans in and clenches her jaw as she speaks, 'I'll say this slowly, you know with the language barrier and everything—'

Low but audible laughter erupts from her table. I feel my cheeks redden but I grit my teeth.

'We didn't write anything about Sophia, and if you go to the headmaster or our parents about this, then I'm pretty sure your parents will be just as interested in what you've been up to, especially when it comes to Aiden.'

My eyes start to water as her words stab me in the chest like a deep sharp knife, catching in between my rib bones.

'Your parents are quite strict, aren't they? Muslim? How would they feel about their only daughter meeting a guy in the woods all by herself? Who knows what happens up there?'

'Nothing happens up there!'

'They don't know that, do they?'

Mollie suddenly rushes over to the table and brushes past me, as if I'm invisible. I always am.

'Did you hear about Lucy?' She finally notices me and stops talking. They all wait for me to leave.

Tears suddenly start streaming down my face and my feet back up, away from this table, away from all of them. I turn and start pushing back through the crowd, exiting the cafeteria at the nearest door I can find. The first bell echoes down the halls. People start pouring out of the lunch room, like a flooded dam. I shift and let them pass around me. I catch Steve's eye as he breezes past me. He walks by himself. He glances up at me, his eyes softer than usual, but he doesn't say anything to me. He just passes me and doesn't look back.

When the second bell rings, I'm still standing there.

I shuffle to my first class and take the first seat in the row. I don't raise my hand when a question is posed by the teacher, I don't offer to share my work, and I don't take notes. I can't stop thinking about their threats. I can't stop thinking about Aiden's parents and what they said on Sunday. I can't stop wondering whether this is all worth it.

When the day finally ends, I go through the usual notions of signing into the UCAS Prep after school class and standing at the back near the door. When the clock hits 3.45, I slide out the door and hurry up to the woods. Light rain hits my face as I leave the building, and mud starts to clot around my boots as I step onto the trail. Turning leaves fall and float through the air around me.

Aiden sits on the bench waiting for me as usual. His hands cradle his iPhone, and he types frantically. I feel my phone vibrate against my hip bone from inside my bag, and know he's messaging me.

When he looks up towards the trail, I wave my arm.

He waves back. Simple. Unburdened. Nothing to lose.

Before I can say anything, his arms are around me, holding me close against his chest. 'Are you OK? I heard about your confrontation with the girls at lunchtime. Why didn't you text me back?'

I pull away from him and shift to the bench. 'Sorry, I was just so angry after. I didn't feel like talking about it to anyone.'

'I'm not anyone though,' he says, squatting down beside me. He hugs my legs and I want to shuffle away from him, but I don't and I don't know why I want that. 'I'm sick of all this drama, and the bullying. I'm sick of Lucy Mc—'

'It wasn't even Lucy today. It was what her friends said about us today that upset me.'

His face scrunches up and he wraps his hands around me tighter. 'What did they say?'

'They all know about us. They know we sneak up to the woods after school at this time. People at school seem to know that we're seeing each other.'

'Well, I didn't say anything to them, or anyone.'

'No, I know, but—'

'And who cares if people at school know anyway?'

I don't know how to react to that, so I laugh but it feels uncomfortable. 'What?'

He pulls himself into me again. 'I don't care what anyone knows about us or what anyone says about us.'

'Of course you don't. You have nothing to worry about. Nothing to lose.' My voice echoes in the woods, in the trees around us.

His fingers drop to the ground, away from my legs. 'Well, maybe it's time to talk to your parents. They might understand.'

'I don't even understand this, how could they?'

'What do you mean by that?'

'Nothing.' How can I explain to him how I'm feeling? How our relationship feels wrong? How if he were Muslim then this wouldn't be an issue? How can I say those words?

'My parents understood and I didn't think that they would?'

I feel the anger again. Flutter in my belly. Tingling in my fingers. Clenched jaw. 'You think your parents were understanding of our relationship? Supportive?'

He stands up, stretches his back and his neck. 'You don't?'

'Forget it, it's just going to turn into an argument.'

'No, you want to say something. I can tell. So say it.'

'I don't want to say anything.'

'Say it.'

'OK, fine! Your parents were visibly freaked out by my appearance!'

'Meaning what?'

'Meaning they're maybe not as supportive as you think.'

'You're being sensitive. You clearly misunderstood—'

'I'm not sensitive, Aiden. I'm realistic! I heard them talking in the kitchen when you went upstairs. Trust me, if I were any different...if I looked like Sophia, or Lucy or anyone else, I would have been accepted no problem into your house on Sunday.'

'You *were* accepted. They were so polite to you—'

'Polite, yes. Welcoming, no.'

'You don't mean that.'

'I do.'

'You don't know them at all. How dare you insinuate they're...they're...racist or something?!'

He's angry. I've never seen Aiden angry before. I never

thought I could make someone angry at me like this. My words did this. I did this. I'm no better than Lucy. My words sting just like hers. The worst part is that Aiden is someone I'd never want to hurt.

'What I'm saying is that if I were white or you were Muslim, then this wouldn't be so much work. Then this relationship might have a future.'

He clears his throat. 'That's it then?'

I want to scream, *No, that's not it! I love you, I don't want this to end!*

But I'm tired. I'm tired of the lies. I'm tired of the truth. So instead I say, 'That's it then.'

This is easier on us both. We're too different. We'll never be accepted as a couple, by either of our communities. It's better that it ends now, than in a year, two years, three years.

He hurls down the trail, back towards the school building. His trainers skid on the wet mud as he turns back towards me. 'Goodbye then, Ulana.'

'Goodbye, Aiden.'

TRINA

I sat beside her.

Waiting.

I needed to know that she was OK. I couldn't leave her. I promised her I wouldn't leave her and I had meant it. I still mean it.

The hospital was really quiet. The rooms absent of emotion, absent of life in some, and absent of the past. Only the present was important. The hallway outside was silent. The occasional footsteps of a passing nurse or doctor interrupted the peace but other than that I heard nothing beyond the doors of Lucy's hospital room. It was just her and me in there, no one else. The nurse had called her mum and while we waited for her, I sat beside her.

Waiting. And talking. We talked for what felt like ages but it couldn't have been that long. It was just new for

227

us – talking, not fighting. It surprised me how easy it was to do that, how easy it was to confide in her, how easy it was to trust her. Then she closed her eyes again, and while she drifted in and out of consciousness, I replayed what happened in the woods over and over in my mind. Her face. Her anger. Her words. Then the screams. Those screams. She was so scared.

One minute she was yelling at me and the next she was on her knees, doubled over in excruciating pain, and begging me not to leave her. She said the words, 'Don't leave me.' I heard them. She definitely said them.

We waited for almost fifteen minutes until the ambulance came. At this point, a small crowd of people had gathered at the foot of the hill, watching as a small team of medics and school staff surrounded us. They'd appeared from behind the large oak tree at the bottom of the trail and stayed there until the PE teacher shooed them away. Back to their classes. Back to their phones. Back to their gossip. This was exciting for them. Thrilling. Maybe even a little fun.

But this was Lucy's life. My life. And now, maybe a third life too – if He…She…It…survives. What do you call a person before it becomes an actual person? Is it too early to name? Has Lucy named her baby yet? I bet it'd be a really girlie name if it was a girl, or something she heard off a movie or an American TV show like Aria or Stella. Or maybe she's waiting until – until – what if it doesn't survive this? What if I didn't call the front office quick enough? I should have directly called the ambulance. But I didn't know what to do. I panicked. I called the school and they called the ambulance. I lost Lucy those precious, maybe even vital, few moments. And if her baby doesn't survive, it will all be my fault.

It was like it was all in slow motion – the medics lifting her onto a stretcher and carrying her down the hill. The rain had lightened but a mist still sat heavy around us and freckled her face with dew. I remember having a strong urge to wipe the rain from her face. I don't know why. I shouldn't have wanted to help her. I shouldn't have wanted to brush the dampness from her cheeks, both from rain and her tears. Why would I have wanted to do that? I hate her.

Well, I thought I hated her.

But now, I don't feel that way. As I sat by her hospital bed waiting for her mum to come, all I thought was, I hope she's going to be OK. I hope her baby is safe. I was worried about her. I still am.

I remember the dirt on my boots as I left the trail. The way the mud clumped around the studs on the bottom of my heels. The little leaf that had got stuck in my boot buckle near the zip. My face after – all red and puffy. The fine hairs around my forehead that stuck to my skin after the rain. I remember her face when they loaded her stretcher into the ambulance. She looked right at me. Her eyes burned into mine. It was like everything changed, in that one moment. We were different. Everything was different.

After they had shut the doors, I watched the ambulance pull away, the brake lights coming on as the van halted to a stop until a teacher moved the students that gathered again. Again, wanting a piece of the excitement, of the thrill, of the fun.

Rhys was there too. He stood beside me at first, his arm wrapped around my shoulders. He asked if I was OK. I didn't know what to say to him. There was so much to say, but no words came out. I'd pushed him away after the party. I didn't return his texts or his calls. I was too ashamed. What we had seemed so long ago. It seemed so innocent, so trivial. It's nothing to me now. Just a tainted memory of a nice summer with a boy I once fancied. I lightly brushed him off and shifted a little away. I don't like people too close now. He took a step back too, then he asked me what I had hoped he wouldn't. 'Is it true? Is she really pregnant?'

'You'd have to ask her,' I replied, but he wanted more from me. I didn't have more to give. I'd told the whole world she was pregnant, yet as I stood there in front of him, I didn't want to share another thing about her without her permission. What I'd done before was wrong. I don't care about her reputation. I don't care if she lost her popularity crown at school, or if her shallow friends turned their backs on her, or if she'd ruined her chances with Rhys – again. I cared about my actions impacting the life that grew inside her.

Rhys kept pushing for more. 'I'm asking you, not her. Did she say anything?'

'No. She didn't say anything about that. But you should visit her in hospital. She's probably feeling really alone and it turns out her friends aren't really friends at all.'

He rubbed his face, maybe clearing the mist from his skin, maybe wiping the last few weeks from his mind. 'So sorry, Trina. I feel like this is all my fault and—'

I hugged him before he could finish and said, 'It's not your fault. Lucy and I weren't exactly friends before you came along.'

'Maybe that will change now.'

Mr Donaldson, the PE teacher, approached me from behind before I could say anything else and offered me a lift to the hospital to sit with Lucy until they could reach her mum. I said no. Why me? Why would she want me there? Why would I want to go there? But he said she'd asked for me in the ambulance. She'd asked for me to go to the hospital with her. And after that I couldn't say no. I didn't want to say no. I wanted to be with her, to hold her hand and tell her everything was going to be OK. And tomorrow we'd figure out the rest.

The drive to the hospital was long. The rain and traffic slowed us down. Mr Donaldson played the radio, and flickered between several stations before eventually deciding on Classic FM. I didn't know what it was. I'd never really heard music like that before. I mostly listened to chart pop, rock, indie, and embarrassingly, the occasional (and secret) love ballad. But not this. This was nice. It soothed me, calmed me a little. While sitting there, I wondered if I'd ever tune into this station again. Me, listening to classical music? Maybe. After—

After...

I still replay what he said to me: 'Don't worry. Your friend will be OK.'

Instead of thanking him or agreeing that she's going to be just fine, I just stared out the window at the rain battering the glass and said, 'She's not my friend.'

She's not – is she?

SOPHIA

I shuffle past people, edging closer to the door, to my escape. I cradle a loaf of brown bread and a two-pint of semi-skimmed milk in my arms. Mum thought it would be good for me to get out the house, get some air, now that I'm not attending school anymore. 'Authorised Absence.' That's what they're calling it. I no longer have to skip classes or hide in the girls' toilets until the bell rings. My avoidance of homework, peers, lunch in the cafeteria, is no longer deemed 'truancy'. I don't feel any different though; my head isn't any clearer, I'm not happier. I feel worse if anything. I feel even more detached from everyone, from everything. From myself. Now I have even more time to replay the past few months in my head, and to text Steve and wait for a reply that never comes.

I don't hear the taunts from my classmates or see sympathetic glances from those who were on my side. But I can still imagine what they're thinking of me at school, what they're saying about me when I'm not there. The silence, the distance, the not knowing.

It's worse this way.

And now, with these discussions about me repeating my final year at school, it's only going to get worse. I can't handle this anymore. I'm so exhausted from crying, from thinking about it. I just want – I want – I don't know what I want, but I know that something needs to change or else...

'Sophia?'

I turn and clip my elbow on the doorframe of the newsagent's.

Mr Mason, my history teacher, stands not too far from me, a bag of shopping in one hand. 'How are you?' He twists his lips into an awkward smile.

I contemplate potential responses to make this exchange less awkward for both of us – maybe 'I'm good, just taking a few days off to recover from the flu.' Is that believable?

He sets his plastic bag down on the floor by his feet and shifts his hand up to his waist. He's getting ready to say something, I can tell. And I already know the general outline of this upcoming conversation. It'll be like this:

'Sophia, do you know you're failing my history class?'

'No, Sir. I didn't know that.'

'Really? Well, do you know why? No, well I do. It's because you don't apply yourself...it's because you don't

submit your assignments on time…it's because you're not smart…or a problem-solver…or an analytical thinker… it's because you fail at absolutely everything you put your name to…it's because—

'Sophia?'

I glance up and see Mr Mason still standing there, tiny creases in his forehead like my dad gets when he's worried about the football score.

OK, here we go. 'Um, I'm OK.' The milk feels heavy in my arms.

'We heard you'd taken some time off. I think that's good.'

'We?'

'The teaching faculty.'

'Oh.' Now everyone knows. Tomlinson must have told his staff why I was no longer attending school, not that they needed to be told. My photos were in their hallways for them to see for themselves. I wonder how many looked, how many recognised my face, how many were relieved it wasn't their own daughter taped up on the wall.

He lowers his gaze and clears his throat. 'Listen, I… just want you to know that I'm really sorry about what you've been going through at school.'

'What do you mean?' I'm trying too hard to sound surprised. I hear it in my voice. The fakeness. High pitch, the inflection at the end. He's probably seeing right through it. I'm not a good liar. I haven't had much practice. Until now.

'Sophia, how are you?'

'Fine.' (Lie)

'Sophia, have you eaten today?'

'Yes.' (Lie)

'Sophia, where's your homework?'

'I forgot it. I'll bring it in tomorrow though.' (Lie)

'Sophia, are you still texting Steve?'

'No.' (Lie)

'Sophia, you have to get over him.'

'I am.' (Lie)

'Don't worry, Sophia, people will soon stop talking about you and the photos.'

'I know they will.' (Lie)

Lie.

Lie.

Lie.

I just can't stop it now. I don't know why I do it. Maybe I think that no one wants to hear the truth, that the truth is too sad for them, too difficult to hear. Because then they'll know what I'm really thinking, how I'm really feeling. And they'll want to help. But they can't.

'I'm obviously aware of what's been happening and I want you to know that you are not to blame.'

My eyes drop to the floor by his feet and I wonder what

supplies he picked up today. I see a newspaper sticking out, and maybe some sandwich rolls.

'How did the meeting go with your parents?'

'It could've been worse, I guess.' I shift to let people pass, and immediately feel their stares on me even though I know they don't know me, or what I've done.

Mr Mason's hand is on my arm now. But it's gentle, comforting. 'Sophia, it might not seem like it now, but this will pass. People get bored of gossip quickly. Just remember that you have a lot of support here at school, even if you're not feeling it from your peers. There are a lot of people there who can and want to help you in any way.'

His words linger in the air, like Trina's. But again, I leave them there, where they belong. Because like her, like my parents, like everyone else it seems, he wouldn't understand. And because I'm too embarrassed to speak about it anymore. He looks at me, eagerly waiting for my response.

I've always liked Mr Mason. He did his student teaching at Birchwood and quickly became one of the more popular teachers. He treats us like we're adults, like we're his friends. I've never seen him yell, or scold us as if we're toddlers having a tantrum. He's well respected. And I like that, which is why I feel so guilty failing his class. Of all my teachers, he's the one I didn't want to disappoint. But I can't help it. His class is in the afternoon, after lunch, after the cafeteria circus where I usually see Steve and his friends, so I can't concentrate. I don't listen. And I don't do the work. I want to apologise, but I can't. I don't know how to say sorry for something that I know I'm doing, for something that's just such a low priority for me. I can't think of anything else right now. I know he wants to help. But he can't. No one can.

'I should go. My mum will be wondering where I am. But thank you.'

'You know where to find me, Sophia,' he adds quietly, nodding his head as if defeated by my actions, or lack of them.

I shuffle closer to the door again. Hand on the knob, I look over my shoulder in his direction but don't meet his eyes. 'Don't worry, Mr Mason. I'm honestly doing much better.'

Lie.

***

'Sophia?'

My head whips back and Ulana's slim frame and loose-fitting head scarf comes back into focus. Then I notice the silver metal table we sit at outside Jo's BusStop, the plastic chair beneath me, the napkin dispenser tugged by the wind, and then finally the cold sharpened by the wind.

'You were totally away with it there.' She smiles. 'Can we go inside? It's freezing out here.'

I nod slowly but suddenly can't remember what question I'm saying yes to. What did she just ask me again? I roll a stone under the ball of my shoe, imagining what it would feel like on my skin, under my skin, inside my skin.

'Sophia?'

'Hmm?'

'Are you OK?'

'Yeah, why?'

'I bet you're glad to be out of school for a few days. Has anything new happened?'

I shake my head and look out past the red Toyota hurling down Schoolhill Road. My fingers grip the coffee cup, pressing into the cardboard sleeve even though it's no longer warm on my skin. It's still full, the contents barely touched. It's my favourite. A sugar-free vanilla latte made with coconut milk. Jo even remembered to make it extra-hot for me. But today it's doesn't taste right. Today, nothing feels right. Everything is alien to me, nothing has any level of familiar comfort. It's new, different.

I look up at Ulana, her eyes actively searching my face for any clue as to why I've hardly said two words to her this afternoon. I know she had a fight with Aiden, but I can't remember if I asked her about it, and I'm too tired to find out. 'Can we go?'

A faint smile softens her face and she nods her head slowly. 'Sure.'

I trudge up the bus steps, my body tired and heavy. I slide the coffee onto the wooden counter, not wanting to toss it in the bin in case it spills out and makes a mess. Jo, the owner, pops up from behind the counter, a sealed box of stirrers in her hand. She smiles at me and reaches for my cup. 'You didn't like your latte today?' Jo asks me, gently shaking it. The liquid splashes up the edges and sloshes around.

I came here with Steve too. When the weather was nice, we'd sit outside and sip our coffees while we made plans for the weekend. He switched between a mocha and a cappuccino, while I always stuck to my latte choice. He added sugar to his. Two packets of brown. Three packets if he got the large size. And we sat there, right where I was just sitting. But I don't remember those moments now. I can't seem to recall our conversations, our weekend plans. I don't remember much these days. Just fragments detached from what's real, and what's not.

The latte cup still sits in Jo's hand, her fingers pressing into the sleeve that I once touched. 'No, it was fine…I mean, it's good…Sorry, I just let it get cold.'

She turns and pops the plastic lid off. 'I can heat it up for you?'

'No, it's fine. But thank you.'

She squints and inspects me, and I wonder if she has a Facebook account. I wonder if she has a son or a daughter at Birchwood. I wonder what she knows. Because she will know something. Everyone knows.

I pick up the bag from the ground by my feet, for once empty of notebooks and papers, and swing the straps over my shoulder. 'Bye, Jo.' I try to smile, but it feels fake on my face. Ulana waits for me outside, her phone in her palm. She frantically types with her left thumb, but when she sees me walking towards her she stops typing and quickly slides her phone back into bag.

'It's just my mum,' she explains. 'She wants to know what time I'll be home.' She feels like she needs to justify why she's on her phone, who she's talking to. She wants me to know that she's not on Facebook. She feels like she needs an explanation for every time I see her with her phone in her hand. My cheeks warm slightly.

We start walking down Schoolhill Road, our shoulders almost touching.

'I hope they expel Steve formally so it's noted on his school records; no university will accept him then, I'm sure. It sounds harsh, but he really does deserve it. What he did to you was so—'

'I don't really want to talk about it,' I say, turning my head away from her. 'I'm sick of talking about it all the time.'

'Oh sorry.' Ulana tugs at her head scarf, her fingers fumbling. She's uncomfortable, I can tell. I make everyone around me uncomfortable.

'No, it's fine. It's just everyone wants to talk about it and I'm sick of being reminded about it.'

'Are your parents trying to talk to you about it?'

'Them, you, teachers and I don't even go to school anymore. I even had one girl come up to me outside Jo's on Monday and tell me how sorry she was and that I should get Steve arrested. I should just stop coming here.'

'Don't. This is your town too.' She pauses then turns to me. 'Can you though? I mean, get him arrested?'

I shake my head. I'm not having this conversation again with her. 'I don't know, but I would never do that.'

'I can't believe that after all this, you still defend him.'

'You wouldn't understand,' I mutter. I walk a little faster, a little further from her.

Ulana jogs a couple of steps to catch up with me. She touches my arm but I shake her off. 'A lot of people want to help, Sophia. You should take the help. You don't have to go through this alone. You can—'

'I don't need to talk to anyone. No one can understand how I feel,' I say, closing my eyes so I can't see Ulana's expression. I don't want to know what she's really thinking underneath all the kindness. Is it pity?

'Then tell me. Please. I want to understand. Sophia, I want to help but you won't let me.'

'You can't help. No one can!'

'You keep saying that, but it's not true.'

'What about my parents? Are they helping? They can

barely look me in the eye. They're embarrassed probably. I've embarrassed them in front of their friends, in front of the neighbours.'

'People will soon get bored of this and move on to something else, something more exciting. That's what happens.'

'No one's forgetting about this! There's new comments every day, more likes, more dislikes. More people know about this each day. I'll never be able to live this down. I'll never be able to live a normal life! These photos are out there and will stay out there for my whole life. Everyone I ever meet will be able to go online and see naked photos of my body…I…I…' The words get stuck in my throat. My chest tightens and my jaw aches as I clench to hold back the tears. 'I can't do this anymore. I just can't. It hurts too much.'

I don't look back to see Ulana following me. But I hear her. She's calling me. I don't turn back. No point. I know what she'll say. And I know what I'll say. Because nothing changes.

LUCY

I unscrunch the paper in my hand and skim the address again. Huntley Road. This is it. It looks different to what I thought it would look like. It looks…normal. Homey. Like a proper family home. I don't know what I was expecting but this certainly isn't it. Maybe a council flat in a large ugly building where the stairwell is open to the outside, and groups of kids hang out, eyeing up all those who don't belong. Maybe I wasn't expecting a house at all, maybe just a room in a relative's house where a family of five are bundled into one room, each stepping over one another as they argue over who left the wet towel on the floor again.

But this isn't it. It's a real house, with a real garden, and a real person living inside.

It's not big. And the paint around the windows is chipping, exposing a rusty hue of tangerine on the surface. The garden is overgrown and a turned over wheelbarrow sits in the corner, likely now used as a pew for Trina as she lights up another cigarette. But soft amber fills the windows, beyond the lace curtains. And smoke billows out the chimney, the dense cloud getting quickly swallowed up by the cold outdoor air. The TV flickers against the glass panel on the door, and soft sounds spill out from the house. The house is much smaller than mine, and tiny compared to my dad's new house. But it looks comfortable. Not completely different to mine in many ways.

My feet ascend the four stone steps up to the panelled door, but my hands stick by my side. It's taken me a little longer to come here than it should have, after what she did. My mum said she saved my life. That I could have bled out or suffered long-term damage if she'd left me. But even when she'd stood over me – as I lay there in the rain, screaming in agony – I'd never once considered that she'd leave me there, like that. Not even when she hurled insults at me, not even when she posted that photo of me at the Family Planning Clinic on Facebook. I never thought she'd leave me out there. Perhaps because deep down I know she's a better person than I am. A better person than I will ever be.

My fist meets the door before I can rethink being there. No answer. I knock again. Still no answer. I can hear the TV on so I know someone is in there. Maybe she knows it's me and doesn't want to answer. I don't blame her. I probably wouldn't answer the door either. I'd probably leave me standing here on the doorstep in the cold.

As I turn to leave, a click from behind turns me. Trina stands in the doorway, in an oversized grey jumper and pink leggings. Her hair is tied back, scraped back off her face, and she wears no make-up. Her usually black-rimmed eyes are fresh and wide, and her unmarked lips are naturally rosy and matte. She looks...pretty. For once.

A half smile fills her youthful face and she moves away from the door. I think she's inviting me in, so I shift forward and wait for her to correct me, to shut the door in my face. But she doesn't. She moves further inside and opens the door wider for me.

Inside, her house smells of cinnamon and apples. Candles line the bookshelves, which are surprisingly filled with actual books. I couldn't picture Trina huddled up on the sofa with a book in her hands, but unless these are her parents', she must enjoy reading. There are far too many on the shelves to be the result of an accidental collection.

'Are your mum and dad home?'

She shakes her head, and glances towards the living room. 'Do you want to sit down?'

I don't want to get too comfortable here, in her house, with her. But my body still aches from the last week, and

I'm still so exhausted that I worry if I stand any longer, I might fall backwards. My fingers fumble to unfasten the toggles on my beige peacoat, struggling with the last button. When I eventually get loose, and slip my arms out, I don't know what to do with the coat. Trina doesn't move to take it from me; she probably doesn't have a coat rack like we do. So I fold it over my arm and follow her into the living room.

School photos and family memories sit upright in thin silver frames on the mantel that surrounds a small fireplace. A large worn-through recliner is positioned in the back corner, slightly too left to be symmetrical with the wall. Trina collapses down onto the shaggy blue rug in the centre of the room and crosses her legs. She leans back onto her hands and stares up at me, waiting. I drop my coat onto the armchair, and fold down into the same position on the floor, mirroring her.

She loops a strand of her hair around her index finger and twirls it. I realise I know nothing about her, and suddenly have no idea what to say. Outside, cars pass beside the house, their engines a welcome distraction. Birds chirp on the trees then fade out, probably getting ready to fly south with the cold weather beginning to set in. A group of kids laugh and scream as they drift past the windows. I wonder if she knows any of them.

'Do you have any siblings or anything?' I eventually ask, finally breaking the silence in the air.

'Nope,' is all she says. This is going to be harder than I thought. Like the house, I don't know what I was expecting. Did I really think she'd open the door and scoop me up into a big embrace? Did I think it would be like the last few months didn't happen and that we could just start fresh and be friends? The damage here was beyond repair, the cracks in this 'relationship', or whatever this is so deep down to the core, where not a piece can be salvaged or conserved for a later time.

'So…it's just you?'

She shrugs. 'It's just Mum and me now.'

'Oh…no Dad?'

She shakes her head.

'So, your dad left you too?'

She nods. 'I don't know where he is.'

'I know where my dad is. But I don't see him as much now. He has a new family now.'

'Oh. That sucks.'

'Yeah.'

She fiddles with a loose thread on her socks. 'I guess we don't really know anything about each other.' She clears her throat, then sets her gaze down on the floor by her feet. 'Listen, um, what I said in the woods and then again at the hospital…please don't—'

'I won't say anything to anyone, I promise.' And I mean it this time.

She nods slowly as if she's trying to decide whether

to trust me or not. I don't blame her. Sometimes I don't even trust myself.

'I'm sorry about posting that photo of you outside the clinic. That was a horrible thing to do.'

Heat builds inside my belly as I remember how I felt seeing that photo, seeing the reaction of my friends, of those around me who didn't know me. A familiar sensation of anger trickles its way back into my blood. 'Yeah, that was really nasty—'

'OK, but what you said about me from the party was pretty nasty too. Especially when you didn't know the whole truth.'

'I was going off your reputation—'

'What reputation?'

'Seriously? "What reputation?" Are you joking? You're not exactly known for your prudish behaviour at school.'

'You're calling me a slut?'

'No...but you have dated quite a few boys at school.'

'Unbelievable! If you're going to come here to insult me, you can leave!'

'Gladly!' I stand up and yank my coat off her bed.

'I should have known you weren't here to apologise! You're so self-absorbed!'

'Why should I apologise? You're just as guilty as I am!'

'I am nothing like you,' she says, standing up to face me. 'You're a bully, Lucy McNeil. And now you've tasted what it's like to be on the other end, you don't like it! People like you are just cowards deep down.'

'I'm a coward?' I laugh, heading down the hallway towards the front door. The smell of apples and cinnamon choke me. 'You're the one who's too scared to tell anyone about what happened at the party.'

'What?'

'You heard me.' I spin round. 'Rather than moping about it, do something. If you're claiming that it wasn't consensual, that you said no, then go to the police.'

'I can't go to the police,' she mutters, her voice suddenly nothing but a whisper.

'Why not? Scared?'

Her face hardens, and the soft youthful expression fades quickly from her face. Her jawline tenses. 'Get out.' She leans in, and opens the door from behind me, the door handle hitting me in the back. A cold breeze rushes in and strikes the back of my coat.

When I step outside, night fighting with the last light of the day, she slams the door behind me. I resist looking back until I get to the front gate. She stands at the window, her frame illuminated from the TV glow. I wait for a moment too long, staring back at her. Then I button up my coat to my chin to battle the cold, and march down her street to the bus stop. As I get closer to the shelter, one glass panel smashed, the shards sitting on the pavement, I suddenly realise that I didn't say any of the things I had intended to say to Trina. None of the words I wanted to say were spoken. Not once did I say, 'Thank you' or 'I'm sorry.'

I didn't even try.

ULANA

'I told you, Dad. I've been going there every week since September,' I mumble, checking my phone screen again. Why isn't Sophia responding to my messages?

My dad paces in front of the dining table. His tall heavy frame shakes Mum's display plates in the glass cabinet every time he passes it. He only paces when he's stressed or thinking a decision over, or both. He grips an A4-sized typed letter in his left hand. His right hand is free to occasionally rub his chin, massage his temples or run through his hair which is now salt and pepper-hued. He stops at the chair closest to me, then sits back down in it. 'So why is the school saying that you haven't been going?'

I slowly put the phone down on the table. 'What? I have been going. Ask for the attendance. You'll see I sign myself in every week. No absences.'

'Every week?'

'Yes…well except this week. But I came straight home that day, remember?' If I'd gone to the UCAS Prep then I'd have been tempted to go look to see if Aiden was up there waiting for me on the bench. And if I had checked, then either he would be there and I'd find that conversation too difficult and probably cry, or he wouldn't be there and I'd still cry. The outcome would be the same, either way.

'So, I'll call the school tomorrow and get this sorted out. I don't want this sort of letter going into your file. Your record needs to be clean for going to university.'

'Dad, my record is clean. Plus I have the best grades in the class. I'll be just fine,' I say, leaning forward and resting my hand on his arm.

He claps it with his free hand and finally breaks into the warm smile I'm used to. 'I'll call the class tutor too, speak to him directly.'

My body is suddenly on fire. 'Why?'

'I want to know why I'm getting this letter, but I also want to make sure you're learning everything you should be. I want you to have a strong application to submit. If this prep class is a waste of time, you stop going.'

My mouth is dry. If my dad talks to the teacher directly, he might confirm that I've been signing myself in every week, but he might also know that I've been sneaking out after about ten or fifteen minutes. What then? How do I explain that? I can't. He'll wonder where I've been going, what I've been doing, and soon, with whom I've been with.

'He's not a real teacher at school, Dad. He's a rep for UCAS, so you won't be able to contact him directly.'

My dad's forehead cracks and tiny thin lines scatter across it. I don't think he's going to let this go that easily.

'But I'll tell him next week that you want to talk with him, and see what he can do.' I pat my dad's hand and he smiles again. 'I'll start dinner with Mum.' I hurry into the kitchen before any more questions arise, and turn the radio on loudly. Fragments of string and wind instruments seep through the speaker into the kitchen, and out from under the door into the rest of the house. My dad always keeps the radio tuned to Classic FM. Anything else he just doesn't understand. Except for the Beatles. He understands the Beatles.

My mum slips in behind me and slides out the spice rack. She starts pulling out the turmeric, cumin, masala. Fluffy powders of orange, yellow and dirt brown. A cinnamon stick lies by the white plastic chopping board, its edges stained with the colours of our country. My dad is last to enter the kitchen. He tenderly touches my mum's shoulder as she sautés the garlic and ginger, then moves to the radio and tweaks it a little louder. He starts on the fish – a whole one too, eyes, head, teeth, too much. Together we cube the fish and simmer the spices, plum tomatoes, chickpeas and onions, until the smells fill the whole house. The steam keeps us in our bubble in our little kitchen, protected from the outside world which, like popular music, we don't understand. I'm safe here in this bubble, in this family. So why would I want anything different? With Aiden, it would be a life so drastically different from the one I've been raised in. It would mean compromising on my beliefs, it would mean sacrificing everything I have for a future that's not even guaranteed to make me happy?

This is why I avoided Aiden for so long. At the time it wasn't difficult for me because I barely knew him. But once we started to open up to each other, once the feelings got stronger, the decision became harder, and soon I couldn't stay away from him. I thought about him all the time, even dreamt about him. So I started talking to him again. I reinitiated it. Not him. He gave me the chance to walk away, before we'd lost any time to it, lost any emotions to it. But I came back, not quite done with what I could never have. And those conversations moved from the classroom to the back of the school, to the woods, to the bench, and beyond. The sadness I felt without him far outweighed the negatives. But this summer changed things for us. The physical distance between us brought us closer. It made me realise that I needed him. That I wanted him in my life. But at what cost?

Now I'd lost him. I'd lied to my parents, snuck around

behind their back, skipped out on after-school activities. For what? A relationship that had ended all by itself. All that risk for nothing.

It's always for nothing.

TRINA

<u>Journal Entry 8: 19.12.2018 – 2018 is almost over, thank God</u>

106,098.

That's the number of people who were sexually attacked in 2016 and reported it.

106,098.

I Googled it. I just wanted to find out how many others felt like me. Even though I've felt alone, I knew I wouldn't be. But wow, I wasn't expecting that number. I can't believe that many people went through what I did, and that they went to the police about it. Now I feel like I've let 106,098 people down. Because I'm not brave like them. Maybe Lucy's right.

I thought a lot about what she said after she left my house last week. In fact, it was all I thought about for days after. 'You're the one who's too scared to tell anyone about what happened at the party.' That's what she said to me on my own doorstep before she left – without saying 'Thanks for saving my life, Trina' or 'I'm sorry for being a complete and total bitch to you this year.'

So what if I'm scared? She has no idea what I went through, what I'm still going through every single day. Every single moment, I'm transported back to that night. I still can't sleep, I'm still barely eating. I've lost weight and now my mum is noticing. I will tell her one day. I want to. She's the only person I can tell about it.

But not yet. Soon.

Mum's calling me right now for dinner, but I'm not hungry. I can't eat, not today. Because I saw Him today. HIM.

I was walking down the high street, counting the contents of my wallet, deciding whether I could afford a new pack of cigarettes – I smoke a lot more now – and when I looked up, there he was. He was on the same side of the street as me, walking fast as if he was late to meet someone. I stopped dead. I dropped a couple of coins that I think landed by my feet. I forgot to pick them up after. Kicking myself about that too. I don't know if he saw me, but he walked right past me as if I was invisible. Right past me! While I stood there, frozen in complete fear, terrified he'd notice me, try to talk to me, try to reach out and touch me, he just strolled by looking so relaxed, so free, so unimpacted. He probably didn't even recognise me. I don't even recognise myself these days. I hardly ever wear make-up, and I try hard to cover up every inch of my body in clothes a size too big. I don't want to draw too much attention to myself anymore. I don't want guys to look at me, to – to – want me. It was my fault last time. It won't be my fault next time.

By the time I got home, I had a gash on my right palm. I must have been clenching my fist so hard that my nails dug into my skin and drew blood. I hadn't even felt it. My hands are still trembling, even now.

I heard a rumour at school earlier this week – for once not about me. It was about a girl in the year below me, Sara something. Pretty girl, reddish hair, huge green eyes. Outside by the chem labs while I was lighting up, I heard a few people from that year talking about a party they went to last Friday – I wasn't there. I never go to parties anymore. I don't like to be around large crowds of people anymore, especially those who are drinking. I don't trust anyone anymore. Not even myself. I'll never ever put myself in that kind of situation again, the kind where I let go, where I trust, where I make stupid naive assumptions about people. No, never again. No one will catch me out again. I'll never be used like that again. So I avoid the parties at weekends. I avoid the crowds, and the risk. Because there's always risk.

It's safer for me here at home. So that's where I stay most evenings and weekends now. These four walls that cocoon me right now are the only thing protecting me. Outside these walls, it's too unpredictable. It's too... dangerous.

Anyway, after this party last Friday, I heard talk about Sara and – and – Him, about how they'd had sex in the barn outside the house. When I heard people talking about it outside chem, I threw my cigarette down and walked right over to them. I was so angry, I could feel searing heat racing through my entire body and shooting out my arms. I thought for a split second that I'd burned myself with my lighter, but I hadn't. I was just that furious, I was boiling over. I screamed at them, told them to stop talking about people behind their back. Then I threatened to hit one of them. I would have too, had the bell not rang. I could feel it in my hand, the quiver, the tremble. I wanted to strike one of them, both of them, anyone really. And when the bell went off, I suddenly couldn't remember how I'd got myself into that state. It was like I was in a trance or something. That's exactly how I felt when He passed me on the street.

All I kept thinking was what if the same thing happened to Sara that happened to me? What if this was all my fault? Because of my silence, I'd let this happen to someone else?

I threw up shortly after that confrontation at school. Couldn't keep my cold lunch down. Everything came up. Tuna sandwich and all. Yuck.

I threw up today too. After I saw Him. This time I hadn't eaten much, so nothing really came up. My chest and throat still hurt from all the dry heaving.

Maybe Lucy's right. I am a coward. I probably won't do anything about it and it'll just happen to someone else again, and then they'll be too scared to do anything, and people like Him will get away with it again and again. Is that what I really want? Is this who I am? Am I the kind of person who'd let this happen to someone else when I could have stopped it, stopped Him? I don't know. I honestly don't know what kind of person I am.

I can't even bring myself to write his name. I don't want him to taint my journal, spoil my thoughts – poison my words. When I can write his name, when I can say it, then I'll know I'm ready. I'll do it. I will. Soon.

Just give me more time, please. Just a few more days, maybe a week, or a…

What if I never do it?

SOPHIA

'Steve?'

I stand in a crowded room of people, the speaker only inches from my feet, the music vibrating against the hardwood flooring by my brown suede flats. Bodies move beside me. Shifting. Swaying. Shuffling to the rhythm seeping out from the black cone, coated in ceramic and metal. They dance as if in slow motion. As if everything is in slow motion. Except me. I'm the only one moving at a normal pace through the crowd. I think I'm moving. Maybe my feet are still.

I don't know. I can't tell anymore.

When I open my mouth to say his name again, my voice gargles out, lost in a sea of spit and foreign sounds. My lips tingle. My tongue feels too big for the inside of my mouth. So I part my lips, and let it hang out a little.

I didn't know it would feel like this.

I only took one pill. Washed it down with a gulp of

cheap newsagent vodka. He said that I would feel relaxed. Confident. Normal again.

But I don't feel normal. I feel…

Weird.

Where am I again?

I look over my shoulder. Left. Then right. A party. That's right. I'm at a party.

Why am I here though?

'Steve.'

Did I say that or think it? I don't know.

I'm freezing all of a sudden. Is there a window open? My fingers trace the goosebumps all over my bare arms, right up to my shoulders, bones sticking out all over. I push into my skin but my fingers just sink in deeper. No bounce. No squish. Just taut skin over sharp bones.

'Steve!' This time it's louder when it escapes my lips. A couple of heads in front of me turn towards me, to see where the voice came from. They look at me like I have two heads. Then they shake their heads and look away, like I disgust them.

The room starts spinning around me. I'm in a tumble dryer whipping round and round, being squeezed out until there's nothing inside me. The floor beneath my shoes start rippling like an ocean wave, bobbing me up and down.

Up.

Down.

Up.

Steve.

There he is, standing in front of me. He's wearing that jumper I bought him. It looks nice on him, brings out the blue in his eyes. I'm now touching it. It's so soft. He holds me by the wrists and pushes me back away from him, but he doesn't let go of me. He's hurting me. No, he's steadying me because I can't stand still. He's helping me. I think.

'What are you doing here, Sophia?'

I reach up to touch the dimples by the corners of his mouth but he jerks his head back away from my fingertips.

'I just want to talk,' I splutter out, pitching forward onto him. He catches me and puts me back onto my feet, dropping his grip from my wrists. 'You won't take my calls. You won't reply to my texts.'

He shakes his head and looks around the room to see who's listening, who's watching.

'They're always watching,' I say, then start laughing.

He scrunches his face up like he's also disgusted by me. 'I got suspended, Sophia. I'm not going to graduate this year. I don't even know whether I'll be allowed to come back and repeat the year. Tomlinson is talking about expulsion.'

'They made me tell. I would never have told, Steve,' I beg, reaching up to him again.

'Leave it be. Go home. You're a total mess. It's embarrassing.' He starts to walk away.

'Don't go!' I only mean to grab his arm, pull him back towards me, into me. But I lunge too quickly, and my hands shoot out too fast, too hard. I grab him by the hair instead and claw at his head. He shields his face from my twitching snapping fingertips, and shoves me gently. But the room was already moving too quickly for me, and I stumble back.

The floor is hard on my elbow, on my hipbone that now juts out from the waistband of my jeans. Laughter erupts all around me. People point while I lie on the floor. No one helps me up. No one extends a hand and supports me to get back onto my feet. No. They point. They laugh.

The floor is sticky, and my fingers where I hold my elbow are warm and wet. When I pull my hand away, I see blood on the tips. I'm bleeding. But I don't feel the pain. All I feel is numb. Cold. Hot. I feel everything. I feel nothing.

I stumble onto my feet and limp to the door. It slams shut behind me, as a burst of cold air slaps me across the feet.

A car pulls up in front of the house. Gravel on the tyres. Stones tremble under the vibrations. From the car. From the music inside. From the heat burning inside my body.

It stops right in front of me, and the engine cuts out.

The door opens, slowly. A tall thin figure emerges from inside. It's cloaked in a dark hoodie, dark jeans, Ugg boots to shield the cold from her toes. Her tummy protrudes, like the bones on my hips.

'Sophia?' Lucy walks over to me, car keys in her left hand. They jingle and clink as she gets nearer to my side. 'Are you OK? You look like you're going to throw up.'

She puts her arm around my shoulder and pulls me towards her car, but I jerk away.

'Sophia, let me take you home.'

Everything around is still shifting, swaying, shuffling.

When she takes another step towards me, I jerk back and start running towards the side of the house, into the woods. I think she's gone but she's behind me.

Lucy stumbles over broken branches, dead crunchy leaves, around stark trees stripped bare from the cold wind. She calls my name. Over and over again. She begs me to stop, to slow down, to wait for her.

But I don't stop. I don't wait for her. I run as fast as I can, as far away from them as I can. Until finally, my feet reach the edge of the road.

But I don't cross. I see them all. Their faces. Their sneers. I know this is high school and there is so much more yet to come, but right now, right at this very moment, I don't want to wait for it to come. I can't wait. And what if when it comes, when it finally comes, it's the same? What if this is it? Are we really that different when we leave these doors at graduation? No. We're the same. We carry the same hate. But this time we bring it out into the world, spreading it. Stretching it out as wide as it can possibly go. Passing it on to each other like a contagious disease. That's what it is. A disease. And we transmit it like the common cold.

I don't want to live in that world. I don't want to get a day older, and know that life will always be this difficult, this cruel, this unchanging.

My body tingles. Butterflies flutter in my belly, diving down and swooping back up like a bird soaring high in the sky. That's where I'll be. Soaring high above in the sky. Looking down at everyone here, fighting with each other, hating each other.

My fingers graze the legs of my jeans, and my whole body trembles. I tip my head up to the sky, and feel the misty rain settle on my skin. Its coolness calms me. And when I open my eyes, tiny white stars sparkle above me. The sky really is so clear here. That's why it's a dark sky reserve, where thousands of people gather at the end of the month for the annual Dark Skies Festival. My mum took me once. We bundled up in our winter coats, mittens and boots, and gazed through telescopes at the vast darkness above us. A universe so infinite that it scares people. But not me. I'm soothed by it, knowing there's so much more out there, beyond all this.

The trees rustle, a cool breeze running through them

spilling out into the road towards me. When it reaches me, I shiver. Goose bumps surface on my arms, and I feel my skin against the thick jumper underneath. I feel everything tonight. Everything is so much softer, harder, cooler, hotter, louder. Everything is louder. The wind in the trees, the distant thumping of music behind me from Lee's house, the rain on the ground. And the car down the road. I hear the car. It's moving fast. Too fast. It's icy tonight. If it brakes, it won't be able to stop.

It won't be able to stop.

I hear Lucy calling my name from behind me. She can't keep up. She won't reach me in time.

When I turn my head, I see the bright headlights coming towards me. And when I step out in front, I don't feel the hate anymore.

I don't feel anything anymore.

LUCY

Posters of her are scattered across the walls of every hallway, every classroom, every locker. No longer do I see the stolen images of a young naive girl. She's been replaced by a smiling, much healthier, vibrant young woman. It's last year's yearbook photo. Her hair is a little longer, curled at the bottom but not enough to be a tight ringlet. More like a loose wave. Like on a summer's day at the beach, when the tide slowly rolls over the next, unhurried and untarnished by the previous one.

The words '#WeAreNotOkay' sit in bold across the bottom of the black and white image. The posters are everywhere. Her eyes – her once youthful, hopeful eyes – they follow me. Down the hall. Into the classroom. Past the cafeteria where I no longer sit.

It makes me angry to see those words.

We.

Are.

Not.

Okay.

Look what we did to Sophia, what we made her do to herself. No, we're not okay. Definitely not okay.

This has been such a quiet week at Birchwood High School. For the first time in weeks, months – no gossip, no whisperings, no tauntings. Just silence. We're in shock. We're in grief. We feel everything. And nothing all at the same time.

I can't even remember a time before this school year, when everything got so crazy. My mind no longer wanders back to the carefree days of camping and sitting out under the night sky. I can no longer remember a time when everything was so much simpler, so much kinder.

When did we become these people?

I never knew Sophia well.

I barely remember her from last year, before she met Steve. All I know is that she was quiet, stayed mostly to herself. She was always with Ulana, and together they floated just a little bit above the rest of us. And rightfully so. She was bigger than this school. Bigger than this life. I just wish she'd realised that. I wish someone had told her that.

She changed a lot this year, after she met Steve. She blossomed into this confident and sparkly person, and at times I envied her. I envied that confidence, her kind nature, her sweet and naive outlook on life.

We.

Are.

Not.

Okay.

Then I see Steve coming out of the headmaster's office. Is he back already? How dare he come back here, not this soon, not after—

'You did this!' I scream at him, running at him until my hands collide with his chest.

He tumbles backwards and slams into the wall. He looks angry at first, his face all clenched up. His hands tighten like he wants to hit me. But then his face softens and I realise that he's been crying too. No, he doesn't get to cry. He doesn't get to feel that emotion, that sadness. He did this to Sophia, to me. I run at him again, this time slapping him hard across his face. He turns away from me, so I raise my fist to strike him harder. But he just takes it. I pull away and stumble backwards, falling hard against the stone.

He stands slowly and smooths his T-shirt. He looks at me, still on the floor, then steps over me. But before he pulls open the door to go back inside, I scream his name again. 'It's yours, you know!'

He freezes, his whole back tensing at the doorway.

I feel a burning in my throat, rising up. I cover my mouth gently in case it's vomit, but it's not. It's words. And that burning sensation, is the truth. Finally. The Truth. 'It's your baby. But you already know that, don't you?'

A small crowd gathers around us, most of them with their mouths agape and their eyes wide. They love this. They're hungry for drama. All of them.

He doesn't even turn around to look at me, to look at the faces of our classmates, of the whole school. He just walks away. Back inside, back to his normal routine, like nothing's changed. But I know it has. No one is that empty inside. Not even him. He knows it too. He feels it too. He's just too scared to say the words.

I'm not.

I'll say them.

WE DID THIS TO SOPHIA.

We're guilty.

Both of us.

Maybe even all of us.

We.

Are.

Not.

Okay.

Light arms grip me from behind and struggle to heave me to my feet. An overpowering smell of neroli, citrus and musk invades my nose, and I stifle a sneeze. Only one person wears perfume that strong other than my English teacher.

Once on my feet, I smooth my uniform and brush off the gravel from the back. Then I turn to Trina who stands close beside me, with my shoulder bag in her hand.

'You OK?' she asks. I nod but my lips start to tremble and my facade starts to crack. She grabs my arm and leads me inside the cold sterile building that no longer seems familiar or comfortable to me. The New Me. I look down at my growing belly, that pushes against the waistband of my grey tights.

We brush past curious faces, turning heads, whispered voices and reach the door of the toilets. Trina glances up and down the hallway, suspicious of everything and everyone, and pulls me inside. She slides the lock across the door and drops our bags by the bin. I bend at the sink and splash cold water on my face and neck. It cools me down but the heat still burns inside me. I hate him. I hate Steve. I don't know what I expected from him. An 'I'm Sorry' hug? A grand gesture where he promises to support me throughout this pregnancy? Maybe just an acknowledgement that he played a role in this, in any of this – the pregnancy, Sophia's bullying, her suicide. Anything.

How can anyone be that cold? That cruel?

Or maybe he's just scared.

I can't fault that. I'm terrified too. And if I had the opportunity, I would run as far away from this as I possibly could.

Trina eventually steps closer to me and leans against one of the sinks. 'So, is it true?'

'Which part?'

'All of it? Is Steve really the father of…of…that?' she says, pointing to my belly.

Rubbing a paper towel across my face, the scratchy texture nipping at my skin, I turn and lean against the sink too. 'Yeah.'

'When? How?'

'Matthew's party in August, where I saw you and Rhys together. I was so upset, so mad at you both. I really thought Rhys and I'd get back together last summer, at least before school started back and when we didn't…I was just so angry, so hurt. And I got drunk. *Really* drunk. And Steve was there, without Sophia. She never came to parties.'

'She was smart.' Trina smiles.

'Smarter than us.'

'Are you going to get an abortion?'

Tears well up in the corners of my eyes, and I place a palm to my face. 'I can't now. I left it too late, I think.'

'Maybe…' She edges closer to me. 'Maybe you did that on purpose without really knowing. Maybe deep down you've always wanted to keep this baby.'

I laugh and roll my eyes. 'No way. I never wanted this baby.'

'Didn't you? Because you would have got rid of it by now if that's what you really wanted—'

'I'm seventeen years old! I'm going to uni. When exactly would I be having this baby?'

'It's a new life for you—'

'I don't need a new life! I already have a life, one that I happen to love and I have no intention of saying goodbye to so I can raise a child all by myself.'

'You don't think you could manage?'

I turn and kick at the metal pipes at the bottom of the sink, the intricate coils turning and looping and getting sucked into the white subway tiled floor beneath us. 'No, of course I'd manage. But the point is I don't want to be wheeling a buggy down the street in my school uniform while people whisper behind my back—'

'No one is whispering or passing judgement.'

'No, but I know what they're all thinking. It was a mistake, and I don't plan to pay for it every day of my life. What will people at school say about me?'

She turns too and stares into the mirror at me. 'Who cares what people at school say?'

'I'm not you, Trina. I care what people think about me.'

'I do too. I'm not immune to gossip. It hurts me too. But I don't see why we have to live our lives a certain way because we're scared about what people will say or think about us.'

'I—'

'Look what happened to Sophia.'

My shoulders suddenly twist and shake, and I curl into my hands, sobbing. Trina places a hand on me and I roll into her. I rest my head on her shoulder and gaze out onto the tiled flooring.

'It's not your fault,' she says, holding me tighter. 'It's not anyone's fault.'

'Have you seen Ulana?' I splutter out.

'No. She hasn't been at school all week. I don't know when she'll be back.'

'Do you think she'll come back?'

Trina releases me and drops her hands by her side. 'I'm sure. She's strong. Like you.'

'I'm not strong.' I lean back against the sink.

'You're stronger than you think.'

'So are you.'

Trina smiles at me and slowly reaches to touch my belly. 'Can I?'

I nod and let her. I drop my chin to my chest and gaze down at the growing life inside me. A smile creeps across my face before I can stop it.

ULANA

'Sophia.'

I speak her name as if she's still here. As if she stands in front of me still. Golden brown hair. Blue eyes. A heart too big for this life.

'Sophia.'

But she can't hear me. She will never hear me say her name again, or anyone else. She will never know how loved as a friend she was and how much she mattered to me.

I failed her.

I knew she was struggling, knew she was having a hard time. But what did I do? I sent her texts, hugged her when her relationship with Steve ended, told off the girls in the cafeteria. But what did I really do to stop this?

Nothing.

I should have told someone. Her parents. My parents. Headmaster Tomlinson. The guidance counsellor.

Everyone. I should have done everything to help her. I had the opportunity to speak up, more than once, and I never did. I thought that it would all blow over in time. But it didn't blow over. Not for Sophia. It got worse for her and I wasn't there to help her through it.

My pillow is damp from warm tears. Hair sticks around my temples and to my cheeks. I tremble, shivering from the dying radiator heat but I don't slide into the covers. I want to feel the cold wash over me, cool me down.

A light tap at the door startles me. Feet shuffle behind it, and the handle presses down but doesn't release. It slowly moves back up into position. 'Ulana?'

My mum doesn't know whether to come in or not. She's scared of entering, timid of approaching me when I'm like this. I wouldn't know how to take to me either.

'It's OK, come in,' I say to my mum from behind the door. I don't sit up, or even look down at the door to see if she enters.

Finally, light trickles in as she edges inside the room. It's only 6.05 p.m. but it's already dark outside. Still winter. Sophia's favourite time of the year. She loved the winter months because she loved Christmas. She loved the music, the lights, the decorations. She'd watch those American movies where families would string lights up on the roofs of large suburban houses in cookie cutter-shaped streets. They'd bicker, like typical families do, but always come back together just in time for Christmas Day. She loved a happy ending.

I wish she'd got one for herself.

My mum clears her throat and starts for the light switch. But she stops, her fingertips on the clip, and drops her hand back down to her side. 'Are you coming down for dinner?'

I wipe away a tear with the back of my hand, and settle further into the damp pillow, deeper into the soft fabrics of the pillowcase. 'I'm not hungry.'

I can hear her sigh at the doorway, and shift weight, her hipbone popping. 'You have to eat, Ulana. I know it's tough, but you not eating and not sleeping and not going to school will make it worse.'

How could it become worse?

What's worse than this?

'I'm not hungry,' I say again, turning over, my back to her. I lightly touch the thin slivers of cracks in the paint. I wedge my thumbnail into one and imagine splitting the entire wall open. Crack it open, shatter the plaster and beams, expose the ugly darkness inside it.

'I'll keep a plate for you anyway, just in case you decide to come down later.'

'Mum,' I say sitting up slowly.

She turns to my voice and her face brightens slightly.

'Thank you. I'm sorry I've been so…difficult this week.' I curl my legs up into my chest and hug myself tightly.

She shakes her head and glances down at her feet. 'Oh Ulana, I am so sorry for Sophia. I sent her parents a card yesterday. I will stop by this weekend with some food maybe?'

I smile and hug my legs closer, so my knees dig into my collarbones and it starts to hurt. My mum really thinks a hot meal will make them feel better. But she's trying. Who knows what to do in this kind of situation? What is the right way to behave?

'They'd like that.'

I feel the phone beside my left hip vibrate and when my mum leaves, I slowly slide it out.

Come outside, I'm here.

I shimmy out the open door and creep down the stairs. My mum is already back in the kitchen, dishes banging against the wooden table. I slowly unlatch the front door and see Aiden standing on my doorstep, his hands shoved deep into his pockets. His cheeks are flushed red from the cold air and a tuft of hair sits across his forehead. His eyes are bright and wide, but they avoid my face. 'You haven't been returning my calls.'

I shuffle further out into the cold, away from the warm house, away from listening ears. Closing the door behind me, I seal the light and heat inside, and stand exposed to the cold and discomfort. 'You shouldn't be here. My dad will be back from work anytime. My mum is inside.'

He finally looks up at me, and I feel the warmth again,

but not from the house. 'I didn't know what else to do. I needed to make sure you're OK.'

'I'm fine,' I mutter, my eyes stinging from the wetness again.

'Ulana, I'm so sorry, I—'

'You should go.' I let my voice soften, and swallow hard. 'I'm so sorry too. I didn't mean to insult your parents.'

'That doesn't matter now. All that matters is us.'

'You don't understand—'

'You keep saying that, but I do. I really do understand. I love you, Ulana.'

I don't know what to say to him. I'm just so tired. I miss her so much. I can't think about anything else, not now. Maybe not ever. I'm tired of the lies, the sneaking around, checking my watch constantly. I'm tired of the nausea and knots that perpetually sit heavy at the bottom of my stomach day in, day out. But most of all, I'm tired of trying to keep away from him when all I want is to be with him. But I can't. Not now.

'Ulana?'

'Dad.'

My dad climbs to the top stair and stands beside me but slightly in front as if blocking me from Aiden. Protecting me from this boy. If only he knew. 'Are you OK? It's freezing out here.'

Aiden wipes his palm on his jean leg. He holds his hand out for my dad to shake. 'Sir,' he says, like he's seen this scene in a movie or TV show and he's acting out a part he thinks is appropriate for this moment.

'Are you OK?' my dad asks me again, reaching his hand up to my shoulder. I nod frantically at him, and touch my cheeks to cool them down.

Aiden is still standing with his hand stretched out-right. He's still waiting for my dad to take it.

Please take it, Dad. Just shake his hand. Please.

My dad nervously glances between Aiden and I, then finally returns the gesture. They lock hands and shake.

'Aiden was just—' my voice hitches '—making sure I'm OK.'

'Ulana and I go to school together,' Aiden says quickly.

'Oh.' I feel my dad relax slightly beside me, as his hands drop down from his hips. 'Well, we should go in, before she catches the cold out here. It's nice to meet you, Aiden.'

'You too, Sir.'

Aiden shifts from the step and turns back down the street. He glances back as I do, and all of a sudden every-thing I want to say to him right there comes flooding back, but I don't open my mouth. I don't say anything.

I just let the door close between us, separating us, maybe this time forever.

TRINA

Journal Entry 9: 22.03.2019

I read a book in Spanish class last year – I know, weird, right? In a class where we're meant to be practising our foreign language skills and we're asked to go home and read a book in English?

Anyway, I weirdly really liked it.

It was a book that had short stories inside it, rather than one big long novel that I'd just add to the list of things that I never get around to finishing. But anyway, this book – I finished it. All of it. And no, I didn't just watch the movie like I did for *Little Women* when asked to do a book study on Louisa M Alcott for English. No, there was no movie for this – OK, I checked that first, I admit it, but I read it. Start to finish. And like I said, I really liked it.

It was supposed to give us insight into Spanish

immigrants in America during the...I don't know...
Seventies or something. And I became transfixed by a
character called Esperanza. What a name.

ESPERANZA

It has a nice ring to it. Better than Katrina. I was terrified people at school would call me Kat like Mum did
sometimes, so I gave myself a nickname before anyone
else could. Trina. It was no Esperanza but at Birchwood
High School, it would get me by.

Anyway, so back to Esperanza. She comes from a big
Latin family, another thing to be envious of – for me,
it's just Mum and I. She was an only child, and I'm an
only child, and now that the man who I occasionally call
'Dad' has gone, well it doesn't really leave us with many
relatives. But Esperanza lives with her parents – both
parents – her sisters, her brothers, her grandparents, all in
this small house in Chicago. And she has these big dreams
for herself. She doesn't want to be pigeon-holed as just
another Latin immigrant, someone whose background,
whose house, whose family will define her. No, she wants
something bigger than that life. And in this book she does
just that. She surprises everyone by becoming something.
And that's what stood out for me. This girl from a nothing family, from a nothing neighbourhood, becoming
someone.

Here, I have the book somewhere on my shelf.

284

That's it. I might read it again one day.

Anyway, I was thinking about that book a lot today, and last year in general. When things were much easier, much simpler than they are now. When all I had to think about was reading a book about an eleven-year-old girl for a Spanish class. When all I had to decide was whether to have Nutella on my toast or Lurpak salted butter before school. When school was a place to hang out in, to meet friends, to catch up on the gossip. Now, it's a place to avoid, to remind me that I no longer have friends, and school is a place where <u>I am the gossip</u>.

I still can't get Lucy's words out of my head, even though it's been a few weeks since she was here. I've thought about our conversation almost every night since. I replay it over and over in my head, and wonder what I could have said, how I could have responded differently. But at the end of the day, I don't know what I could have done differently. Because I know now it's nothing that I did, so that means there's nothing I could have done to stop it.

Lucy called me a coward. She told me I was scared. And for days, weeks, I believed her. Maybe I was a coward. Maybe I was too scared to do anything about it. But then that book came to my mind (probably because it's actually the only book I've ever read and finished from cover to cover all by myself, so maybe that's why it sticks out in my head during this time). This book – that girl, Esperanza, was she scared? I'm sure she was. She was eleven and living in a different country where people thought she was weird and spoke in a funny language. But was she a coward? No.

Am I?

Not today.

Today I am not a coward.

Today I said his name out loud in front of the mirror, and I didn't cry. Today I write his name.

CRAIG

Today I went to the police station.

I waited until the final bell, got dressed after PE – which I actually participated in today thank you, broke a sweat too – and walked there.

It was bigger inside than I thought it would be. The walls were a stark sterile white like the hospital where I sat with Lucy. The chairs in the waiting room were the same too actually. No framed pictures on the wall. Same water cooler in the corner. Same fake potted plant in the middle of a white plastic folding table meant to serve as the 'coffee table'.

Police Station = Hospital

Both places for help, I guess, if you think about it. So maybe they should look the same.

I only had to sit in that waiting room for ten minutes before a female officer came and asked me to follow her back behind the counter, into the main hall. Desks, littered with stacks of files and papers white as the walls, mugs of cold coffee freckled with cooled milk deposits, ballpoint pens, paper clips. Much like my teachers' desks.

School = Police Station = Hospital

She told me I needed my mum there but I lied and told her I was already eighteen. And then she asked me why I was there. Of course, I knew she'd ask me that. It's a simple question – why was I there? She wouldn't exactly be a great police officer if she didn't ask me why I'd just walked into the police station asking to report a crime. It was then that I thought about getting up and leaving. Telling her that I'd changed my mind, or forgot what I was going to say, or that I had nothing to say at all and that I was just here wasting her time on a dare. But then I thought about a girl similar to me in a way. Maybe in many ways. A brave girl.

No, not Esperanza.

I thought about Lucy. And what she's going through. What I could have been going through had a condom not been used by him. I could have been Lucy. It could have been me at the Family Planning Clinic that day. It could have been me on that hill, bleeding, needing an ambulance, begging for help. Begging someone – not just anyone, but my worst enemy – not to leave me alone.

So I recalled that entire night, that party, upstairs in the bedroom. I told her everything. I even told her what

I wore that night, and that I was drunk. But she didn't seem to care about that, and I thought she would. She just said, 'If you said no, then you didn't give your consent. And it doesn't matter what you were wearing, or that you had been drinking. What happened to you wasn't consensual. It was against your will.'

And it was. I didn't give my consent. I said no. She wrote it all down on a piece of paper, asked me to sign and date it, and told me to go home and tell my mum. She said she would take care of it. That HE would never be allowed to do this to anyone else again.

When I left the police station, I started to worry a little. What if he denies it? What if he says I'm the one who's making it all up for attention? What if everyone says that I 'asked for it'? That I caused it, let it happen?

Again, I thought about Lucy. And how I'd blamed her for everything. She didn't cause <u>this</u>. She didn't let <u>this</u> happen. And neither did I. It wasn't what I wore, what I said, what I drank, that I even drank at all. It wasn't my make-up, or my hair, or that I flirted and maybe led him on. It wasn't any of that. It doesn't matter what I wore, what I did. All that matters is that I said NO. This is my body. And I didn't consent to what happened to me at that party. And by not doing anything at all, I could let what happened to me, happen to someone else. I know now that it's OK to be scared. But it's not OK to be a coward. Life is too short to not be brave. Life is too short.

I still think about Sophia sometimes.

I think we all do.

I wonder what her last thoughts were that night, whose face she saw in her mind if anyone, if she texted her parents right before, what she felt – what she must have felt to do that.

I hope I never feel that alone.

I wish I'd confided in her. Then maybe, she would have done the same and we could have been there for each other.

I wish so many things had been different.

I'm sorry, Sophia. I'm so sorry.

LUCY

Pink balloons rock gently in the breeze beside the window Mum's just cracked open. The weather forecast had been cloudy with partial rain this afternoon so we decided last night to move the baby shower indoors. But now the sun shines bright outside. Mum was up most of last night stringing paper lantern lights from the corner of the dining room to the edge of the living room, wrapping baby pink tissue paper around the legs of the table, and tying ribbon onto mason jars filled with creamy white votives. Their flames flickered now in the soft wind.

The downstairs has been completely transformed from its usual state of strewn pillows, empty Diet Coke cans, dirty dinner plates and celebrity magazines boasting the newest diet trend of the season – the Bee Pollen Smoothie diet, the DASH diet, Keto Cure. The old me would've bought into all of those at one point; now I have different priorities. Now I see things in a new light, perhaps in a clearer light. To me, anyway.

I was angry at Cara, Lily and Mollie for a long time after the pregnancy came out. I thought they'd judged me, that they'd turned away from me when I needed them the most. But in truth, they were shocked and confused, just like me. I'd shut them out as I had a lot of people. And now as they sit here in my living room, drinking pink lemonade from pink striped paper straws and gossiping about celebrities who've just had babies with their co-stars, I realise that I'm not alone in this after all. I've never been. I just didn't know that, or trust that. And maybe once they go off to university and start their own lives away from Birchwood we'll lose touch gradually, slowly drift apart like branches in a river. But maybe we won't.

'You OK?' Mum asks, nudging me away from the dining table.

'Yeah, great.' I refill my lemonade tumbler, slightly overdosing on the amount of pink in this room, and rejoin my friends on the sofa.

Mollie pops up and wanders back over to the food, while Lily smooths down the edges of her mint green tea dress.

'Pretty dress,' I say, actually meaning it.

'Thanks. H&M.'

'I haven't been in there in ages.'

'You should. They have a nice children's section.' She

sips her lemonade, then dabs her coral lipstick with her napkin. Pink, of course. Everything here is pink.

Cara turns her head back to the table and I wonder whether she's eyeing Mollie at the sugar end of the display. She never could turn down a caramel eclair. But she whips back to me, and then again towards the table. 'Luce, your mum?'

I feel a big smile stretch across my face. 'Yeah, she looks amazing, right? She's been doing really well the last couple of months, ever since I told her about this one here.' I gesture to my growing belly, my fingers caked in icing sugar from the eclair I had just polished off. Best thing about pregnancy: indulging in every food craving. I mean, second-best thing about pregnancy, of course. The first is seeing Annabel's little face as she enters this world. Annabel Sophia McNeil. I haven't told anyone yet. I want her name to be a surprise. It was a surprise to me too. I finally succumbed and picked up one of the many baby name books my mum had bought me and before I'd hit the B names, I saw 'Annabel'. One of the passages in the books associated it with 'Love', 'Grace', 'Beauty' and 'Favour'. It's also a variant of Anna, my grandmother's name. She died when I was seven, but my mum talks about her often. A black and white photo of her with my grandfather at a disco in Perth sits in a copper frame in my mum's bedroom, which she now sleeps in. Gone are the nights passed out on the sofa with the remote control in her hand and an empty wine glass on the floor by a fallen pillow. This pregnancy – Annabel – has changed everything, for all of us.

I don't know when it was that I decided to keep her. I can't exactly pinpoint the moment I made the biggest decision of my life. It was as if one day I'd woken up knowing that I'd give birth to her and raise her, like it was never a decision at all but more of a sudden realisation. And then I started telling people. My mum first, then my dad, Auntie K, teachers and friends at school, neighbours. I even found myself making a joke that I couldn't drink coffee for another few months at Jo's BusStop Cafe by the school while proudly pointing to my swollen belly. It suddenly became not just acceptable to be pregnant, but just a part of who I am. I'm not just Lucy McNeil, high school student. I'm Lucy McNeil, Annabel's mum. And I'll be just that in every sense of the word, because I owe that to her. I owe that to myself. I'm going to be a good mum. And I don't just tell myself that at night to calm the nerves. I think – I know – I actually mean it.

I'm going to be a good mum.

'What are you smiling about?' asks Cara, playfully nudging me.

I shake my head and merely rub my belly.

'Love your mum's new haircut. She should totally set up a profile on one of those dating apps!' laughs Mollie, as she plops down in the sofa beside me, eclair in her hand.

'One day, definitely. We'll make sure she does. She's cute for her age, right?'

'I'd date her,' shrugs Lily, peeling off the armchair to skip the song on my iPod.

'You'd date anyone,' mutters Cara, leaning into me.

'Oi, I heard that!'

Taylor Swift's new song blasts from the speaker that perches on the bookcase next to a gold-rimmed frame that up until last month used to hold a photo of my dad. Now a photo of my first scan rests inside, not quite big enough to fill the 5x7 frame.

'Is Trina coming today?' asks Cara, looking around.

'She'll be here soon,' I nod. 'She's picking up the shower cake from Frederick's.'

Mollie pulls half an eclair from her glossy sugar covered lips. 'There's cake? Oh no, why didn't anyone tell me?'

'You can have both,' I laugh, gripping my stomach. 'Ow.'

'What's wrong?'

'She's just kicking.'

'She wants cake,' says my mum, walking past.

'She's not the only one,' sighs Mollie.

'Trina's coming up the drive now,' calls my mum, peeling back the lace curtain.

I slowly stand, still uncomfortable from Annabel's kicking, and reach the door before Trina has had a chance to ring the bell.

She stands on the step, hands empty.

'No cake?'

'No hug?' she laughs.

Wrapping my arms around her, I see a familiar figure shuffling up the driveway towards us. My throat suddenly feels dry and I no longer feel Annabel kicking.

Trina pulls away from me and bites her lip. 'Guess who I ran into?'

Steve continues the slow walk up to me, then stops slightly behind Trina. His hands are full with a rectangular white box wrapped in a pink satin ribbon. *More* pink. He smiles, a forced smile, and holds out the cake to me, but I don't take it.

He looks different today. He's wearing a smart collared shirt in pale blue plaid, and ironed trousers. His shoes look like they've been polished to a shine by his mother. He clears his throat. Then he clears it again.

Trina looks away, feigning interest in my mum's garden gnome that looks like Mick Jagger. I think that's why she bought it. 'Actually I think I might just go inside and see if your mum needs any help.' She scoots in, leaving us alone on the doorstep.

He leans in. 'Um…you have every right to just shut the door in my face, but I just wanted to say how sorry I am for how I've acted this year to you—'

'To Sophia too?'

His jaw clenches and the cake box tilts slightly. 'Especially to – to—'

'Sophia. Is it hard to say her name?'

He nods and that's when I see them; the tears in his eyes. My shoulders soften and a fluttering in my belly draws my eyes down. This is about her now, not us, and not the past. I have to stop pointing fingers at everyone else and accept my part in it too.

I inch the door away from us, opening it wider.

He takes a slow deep breath. 'I can come in?'

'It's a full house in there,' I mumble, shrugging my shoulders. 'Just women "ooh-ing" over an unborn baby.'

'I know. I'd still like to come in, if that's OK.' He smiles at me and this time it looks genuine. I suddenly remember the Steve I once knew, the Steve I became close friends with, the Steve Sophia once knew. He can't erase the last year of our lives, the last year of Sophia's life. But he's trying. It's a start.

'Yeah, sure.' I hold the door out and he walks through, cake still gripped in his hands. Probably squished by the way he's holding it. I slowly close the door and hear Steve's voice booming over the end of the Taylor Swift song. 'Whoah. There's a lot of pink in here.'

ULANA

I thought I saw her today. Her face in the lunch crowd, her ponytail bouncing up and down in PE, her long outstretched fingers sliding a scrunched-up portrait of me across the table in biology when she should have been focusing on the whiteboard. I always think I see her. But I never do.

A couple of months have passed already but this isn't getting any easier. I'm still so confused about what happened, why it happened, and why I let it happen.

My phone beeps from under the pillow, and I think it might be Trina or Lucy. They text me now. Lucy invites me out for a tea after school, Trina asks if I'm OK. I didn't really know Lucy until this year, until…everything happened. But she's different now. Everything is much different at Birchwood.

Another beep fills my empty room, void of any light from the lamp. I raise the screen up to my face and for a split second, I think I'm going to see Sophia's name. One of her old messages.

Do you want to come over to watch a movie this weekend?

Have you listened to the new Ed Sheeran song yet?

Do you want to go shopping on Saturday?

Have you done your biology homework yet?

Steve isn't texting me back. Is he with Aiden tonight?

I kept all of our old text threads, and I probably always will. But I might delete the ones from the past couple of months because that's not her. That's not the Sophia that I knew. That was a very different Sophia. One that stepped out into the middle of the road to end her life.

That's not my Sophia.

But it's not her on my phone screen. It's Aiden. He also texts me a lot.

I'm downstairs. Can you come outside for a minute?

I rush to my window and peer down. A hooded figure stands in front of my house, at the bottom of the stairs leading up to the front door. I know that sweatshirt. I know that stance.

I won't ring the bell. I just want to see you for a second.

The hallway is empty so I creep downstairs, avoiding the fifth stair which creaks. My feet hit the last step, softly landing on the carpeted flooring at the bottom. I look back at the closed kitchen door and hear a clash of ceramic. Mum is setting the table for dinner. I glance back one more time before turning the Yale lock so it clicks open. A gush of air rushes in.

Aiden stands, a couple of steps from the top, his hands in his pockets. His face immediately softens when our eyes meet. 'Sorry, I know I shouldn't be here again. And I definitely don't want to get you in trouble. I just didn't know what else to do. You weren't at school again today. I wanted to make sure you're doing OK.'

I step out into the warm early evening in my bare feet. 'I'm fine. What's been happening at school lately?'

'This anti-bullying campaign is really blowing up. Did you see how many followers Birchwood's page has now? It's crazy.'

'Yeah,' I whisper, playing with the fabrics at the bottom of my sleeves.

'They're filming for the YouTube campaign over the next week. Almost everyone's signed up for a spot. Will you come? Will you join in?'

I laugh and rub my forehead, warm tears stinging my cheeks again. 'It's a bit late now, isn't it?'

'I don't think so.'

'Well, I do.'

'No, Ulana, it's not. Maybe it is for Sophia, but not for other people.'

His words pinch my insides and I know deep down, he's right. It's not too late. Not for real change. Maybe this is our opportunity. Maybe today's my opportunity for change. 'OK. I'll be there.'

He smiles and reaches into his back pocket. Still smiling, he holds his arm out to me and slowly uncurls his palm. Inside are tiny yellow buttercups. Yellow was Sophia's favourite colour too.

'Are those from the meadow behind school?' I ask him. He nods.

'Thank you.' My voice is no more than a whisper between us.

'Do you need anything? I mean, I'm here for you if you need anything.'

I nod and hold out my hand for him to join me.

Aiden steps up beside me and hands me the buttercups. His fingers linger a little longer on my hand and I bite my lip fighting back the tears. He holds out his arms and I collapse into him, like he's a part of me. I know the buttercups are getting squashed as he holds me tight, not letting go, but I don't care. I don't want to move. I feel safe here. I'm where I should be.

Inside, my dad's voice stretches out from the kitchen.

'I should go,' Aiden says, sliding his hands down my arms. He lets me go and takes a step away from me. 'Can't let your dad see me again.' He glances over my shoulder into the house, then leans in and kisses me gently on the forehead. His lips are warm and familiar. He pulls away and turns to leave.

'Wait,' I say, taking his hand. I lock my fingers into his and tug him inside with me.

'Ulana...' He tries to pull away but I keep him close to me, leading him further into the house.

We stand at the kitchen door, my parents' voices soft and muffled.

'What are you doing?' he asks, tiny creases spreading across his forehead.

'Something I should have done a long time ago. I'm sorry I didn't.' I push the door open with my hand.

'Ulana? I'm glad you're joining us—' He stops when he sees Aiden behind me and quickly rises from his chair.

'Dad, you remember Aiden?' I stutter, my lips trembling.

My dad nods, 'Yes, I remember your friend Aiden.' He glances between us, waiting for one of us to explain more. I feel my mum behind me, the smell of her perfume in the air around us. It smells like the flowers from home. Oleander and hibiscus. I realise then that both of these things are important to me – that *both* Aiden and my family are important. Both him and my family feel suddenly connected. My relationship with religion and my relationship with him give meaning to my life, and with everything that's happened over these past few months, I don't feel like I should have to choose one over the other anymore. Both are a big part of me. Both should have a place in my life. As difficult as it will be, I know now – I see now – that that's not an impossible task.

'Mum, Dad, I want Aiden to stay for dinner tonight.'

My dad's brow furrows and he looks at my mum who stands beside him, plate and tea towel in hand. She's setting the table for dinner, but she doesn't put the plate down. She continues to hold it, as she flickers her eyes between us and Dad. 'Ulana—'

'I'm not asking to bring him upstairs to my bedroom. I understand we can't be alone together under your roof. I will respect your wishes. I always have. I'm just asking if he can join us for dinner because I'd like for you both to get to know him.'

I glance at my mum. She doesn't seem angry to see Aiden standing here, beside me. She doesn't even seem surprised. She clears her throat, and eventually parts her lips to speak. 'Are you hungry, Aiden?'

Aiden nods quickly, a small smile creeping across his face.

She places a firm hand on my dad's shoulder, as if to soothe any unspoken concerns. He looks up at her, then back to me.

'Good. I'd better set another place at the table then,' she says.

I follow my mum into the living room to get the extra dinner set for Aiden. 'You're not angry?' I whisper to her.

'Of course not. We trust you, Ulana. We always have.'

I wrap my arms around her and rest my cheek on her

chest, the scent of oleander getting stronger. She smells of apricots in the summer. I hug her tighter.

'Besides, at least now you don't have to sneak around with him.'

I pull away, my cheeks feeling warm. 'How do you know—'

'Ulana, I'm your mother. I know you very well. And I also remember what it feels like to be seventeen.' She smiles. 'Now come on, we'd better get in there.'

'Is Dad angry?'

'You're his only daughter, and you just brought a boy home. Give him some time. But I think once he gets to know him, he'll like Aiden a lot. We both will.'

When we return to the dining room, Aiden and my dad are talking, just about football. But they're talking.

A soft silence washes over the table when we sit down. I bite my lip, wondering what to say. Then Aiden clears his throat. 'So I heard you like the Beatles, Mr Alami?' he says, leaning in.

A wide grin spreads across my dad's face as he launches into an animated conversation about the *Sgt Pepper* album.

I pull out the squashed buttercups from my pocket, and set the yellow flowers down next to my silverware. I smile – Sophia would enjoy this story.

TRINA

<u>24.06.2019 – Last Journal Entry!</u>

Well this is it.

My last journal entry.

I am officially eighteen years old and (self-deter-minedly) now too old to be writing in journals anymore.

Besides, I don't want to keep the journal from this last year. I don't want the reminder of what happened, what went wrong, what we did, what we didn't do, what we should have done.

I don't want to be reminded of how much I blamed myself for what happened to me, of how much it changed me. I don't want to see his name again, as happy as I am that I had the courage to write it down, to speak it, to recall it at the police station. I never want to see him again. I don't think anyone will for a long time. Turns out it wasn't just me at that party, or before, or after. I wasn't alone.

I never was.

This journal isn't me anymore. Sure, I still have those thoughts every now and then in my mind – the guilt, the self-blame, it's only natural – but I don't need them written down. It will never be forgotten. We will never forget Sophia Greer.

Birchwood is a very different place now. The school's anti-bullying campaign really took off. Teens across the country took to Twitter, Facebook, YouTube, any social media platform they had access to, and advocated for a better school climate in every building – for a better future. We filmed a documentary for YouTube last month, which got over ten million hits and is still being viewed today. It's even being shown in some high schools throughout the country, as a way to start conversations between students about bullying and social media trolling.

Everyone from the school was there on the day of filming, so much so that the faculty had to expand it over three days because we just couldn't fit everyone in on one day. Everyone showed up. Everyone had something to say. And even if they couldn't verbalise how they really felt, they simply held up a pasteboard that showed Sophia's face. Holding up that board proved they had a voice and they weren't willing to sit quiet. Even Ulana came on the first day of filming. It was hard for her, but Aiden was there. She stands in front of a slideshow of Sophia, of all of us, of teens across the world, along with the words, '#WeAreNotOkay'.

And yes, even Steve came. And Lucy. And on the day, after everything that happened, no one gossiped or pointed fingers, or whispered behind their backs. Steve started a Facebook page for Sophia after the documentary. He's raised over ten thousand pounds for the Anti-Bullying campaign. I don't know how I feel about that, but it's not for me to judge. It's not for any of us to judge or question. We don't have the right to do that when it comes to other people's lives.

I see Ulana a lot now. For the first time since we were kids, I've been spending time at her house again. It's nice to be a part of her life again. I missed her. She had a hard time after Sophia's accident – can I call it an accident? That's what the newspapers called it at first, no one wanted to say what Lucy said she saw that night. That Sophia didn't accidentally stumble drunk – drugged – onto the path of an oncoming car, on an icy night. Lucy said she stepped out in front of it, calmly, intentionally, without a doubt in the world. People said she was lying, just trying to get attention through the whole 'I was there. I saw it.' But I believed her. Everyone who knew Sophia, who witnessed the hell that was this school year, knew Lucy was telling the truth. And then everyone believed her, even her parents, even Steve, even the school. And then the anti-bullying campaign grew from that, until everyone in every school knew the story.

But Ulana is doing better, much better. She got her place at Oxford. In fact, they offered a scholarship which I think means she gets to go to university for free, which is kinda cool.

Speaking of university – and don't laugh because I remember exactly what I said, that further education is for people who read William Shakespeare and colour-coordinate their school folders – but I'm actually planning to go too. I left school at the end of December and started an access course at the local college. I still have another year left – I didn't get the best grades at Birchwood, surprise! – but in another year, assuming I keep up the grades I'm getting now, which are really good, then I'll be joining those girls at university. You know, the ones who drink tea in the afternoons and season-coordinate their wardrobes :)

BUT, I will never own a pen with a fluffy thing on top. However, I do now own a copy of *Romeo & Juliet* by William Shakespeare. Yes, thanks to Lucy and her birthday present to me, I am now one of those people who read Shakespeare! :)

So, Lucy – bet you never thought I'd be writing about her like this in my journal. Yep, we are officially friends. More than friends, actually. We see each other almost every day. She had her baby girl at the end of May and called her Annabel Sophia McNeil. She has light golden hair with flecks of dark brown, red rosy cheeks and the bluest eyes that I have ever seen. She's beautiful. And Lucy is already an amazing mum.

I knew she would be.

And she doesn't regret bringing Annabel into this world – not for a second. Yes, it's changed her life forever. Yes, she has to make new decisions for a future that she now shares with another person. But this other person is just incredible. And I've never seen Lucy so happy, and so sure about anything before.

Sometimes she and Annabel meet me after class in the centre of town. We get the bus to the beach and walk along the sandy shores, throwing stones into the lapping tides until we hear the drop. One day, Annabel will be big enough to throw her own stones. But right now, we throw one for her, and we make a wish for her when we do.

And when Annabel's fast asleep in her cot that sits beside Lucy's bed at her mum's house, we sit downstairs and watch a movie together, or paint our nails and talk about everything – music, clothes, even boys. In fact, she's now become the only person that I can really talk to about anything. I confide in her and she confides in me. And we trust each other, and we trust this new connection we've found, even if it blossomed from rocky, unsteady, often sharp, ground.

Who would have ever thought, eh? Lucy and me: Best Friends. I can't believe how much I once hated her. So much so that it became ingrained in my every step, my every moment. I woke up hating her. I went to bed hating her. But if I've learned anything from the past year, it's that HATE is a strong word. And I'd like to think that I'd never use that word again. I don't need to.

So here we are. Lucy and I. Hanging out together, laughing together, supporting each other. I never used to think that anything was permanent. I thought everything changes because eventually people leave – they move on, or they change their mind, or they just give up. But I see now that some things are permanent, like friendship. Friendship doesn't leave us behind.

I'm going to play Dad's old CD later tonight, the one I found in the attic. I think I'm ready to hear it now. I think I'm ready to be me again.

If you are impacted by any of the issues raised in this book, please don't be afraid to ask for help.

Join the Wear Blue campaign in November 2019 and support anti-bullying efforts in schools. For more details on these issues, visit http://www.bullying.co.uk/

Acknowledgments

I'd like to thank the incredibly talented team at Peters Fraser & Dunlop, HQ, and HarperCollins, especially Silvia Molteni, Clio Cornish, Anna Baggaley and Hannah Smith.

To Dr Liam Murray Bell at the University of Stirling, Cherise Saywell, and my class peers for renewing my love of writing fiction. And lastly, thank you to my family – my parents and my brothers for supporting me regardless, and my sister who always gets lumbered with the task of editing my first drafts!

ONE PLACE. MANY STORIES

Bold, innovative and
empowering publishing.

FOLLOW US ON:

@HQStories